Doug Simpson is a retired Certified Public Accountant. He lives near Lake Whitney, Texas, where he writes and tends to his community-based market garden operation.

To Mitchell, Sadie Rose, Luke, and Charlotte.

Doug Simpson

A WALK WITH BUDDY

The Appalachian Trail Adventure

AUSTIN MACAULEY PUBLISHERS™
LONDON · CAMBRIDGE · NEW YORK · SHARJAH

Copyright © Doug Simpson (2018)

All rights reserved. No part of this publication may be reproduced, distributed, or transmitted in any form or by any means, including photocopying, recording, or other electronic or mechanical methods, without the prior written permission of the publisher, except in the case of brief quotations embodied in critical reviews and certain other noncommercial uses permitted by copyright law. For permission requests, write to the publisher.

Any person who commits any unauthorized act in relation to this publication may be liable to criminal prosecution and civil claims for damages.

This is a work of fiction. Names, characters, businesses, places, events and incidents are either the products of the author's imagination or used in a fictitious manner. Any resemblance to actual persons, living or dead, or actual events is purely coincidental.

Ordering Information:
Quantity sales: special discounts are available on quantity purchases by corporations, associations, and others. For details, contact the publisher at the address below.

Publisher's Cataloguing-in-Publication data
Simpson, Doug
A Walk with Buddy: The Appalachian Trail Adventure

ISBN 9781641823357 (Paperback)
ISBN 9781641823364 (Hardback)
ISBN 9781641823371 (E-Book)

The main category of the book — FICTION / Action & Adventure

www.austinmacauley.com/us

First Published (2018)
Austin Macauley Publishers LLC
40 Wall Street, 28th Floor
New York, NY 10005
USA

mail-usa@austinmacauley.com
+1 (646) 5125767

Chapter One
Unspoken Reasons

Seclusion is the heartbeat of backcountry living. No one is present to encourage, distract, display affection, or lend a helping hand. White noise is missing in wilderness solitude. Routine sound originates with me: hard breath, dog tag clink, bear bell jingle, twigs snap, leaf rustle, and boots crunch on earth or scrape against rocks. All noise that fades with conscious thought as feet move along the passage to the next terminal on the path.

Backpackers end wilderness hikes because they neglect to train their body to withstand physical punishment in the early days. I expect most call it quits because they're not equipped to deal with mental isolation. Thirty minutes. One hour. One day. Two days. One week. One month. When does the stillness of the forest—the loneliness of the climb, and the rise and fall of the trail silence a mind and send an individual running home?

I am asked what drives a person to walk away from civilization to suffer wilderness unknown by themselves for days, and then weeks and months. How can I respond? Backpackers carry unspoken reasons into the wilderness.

What prompted me to leave well-known safe harbors to confront the unknown wilderness by myself from September to November in 2013 to walk The Appalachian Trail for 520-miles? Hiking the Appalachian Trail is the last endurance objective I set for my fifties. I hiked the Grand Canyon top to bottom and returned the same day; finished the 200-mile Seattle-to-Portland bike ride under 10 hours, ran a marathon in under 3:45 hours; and now I plan to hike the Appalachian Trail from Springer Mountain, Georgia to Mount Katahdin's, Baxter Peak.

During the summer of 2012, I closed the book on a worthwhile, two-year turnaround project for a solar energy corporation. The job was hard. The work was fun. I represented an accomplished group of investors and a solid team of clever employees, including my son. This business success gave me a gift: time. I changed my life with this opportunity. My focus shifted from work to family and friends. I set my daily schedule to share every available moment with my adult children and my new grandson. Time spent running with my wife and father around Town Lake was a preference. When I didn't run with loved ones, I trained with my friends; jogging the streets of downtown Austin early in the morning or late in the evening.

Several days a week, my dog, Buddy-Boy and I slipped out my front door to run the rock-laden, mountain bike trails behind my home. Buddy and I quietly prepared to walk the Appalachian Trail together, from Springer Mountain, Georgia to Katahdin, Maine. I planned to start this pilgrimage when I ended my marathon career on February 17, 2013, running 26.2 miles to complete a competitive six race series in Austin Texas.

Gifts of time have limits. Life circumstance—not plans—dictate how I use this endowment. A voice message left by a hospital employee in Kansas waited for me when I finished a Saturday morning run with my father in September 2012. When I returned the phone call, a nurse advised me my mother was their patient and her prognosis was terminal.

"Mr. Simpson, if you wish to say goodbye to your mother, you will need to hurry."

When my children were young, my mother made a heroic choice to take it upon herself to bestow the best life possible to my younger brother and his son; an adult and a child crippled by daunting mental and emotional challenges. I decided early in our family life to remove my wife and children from this atmosphere to safeguard our children's innocence. I accepted this decision for my children's safety, but I was never proud of the choice. Several options existed to deal with this family problem. I chose the easiest for me, instead of the best for everybody.

Father, husband, business man, and son of divorced parents. These were roles I led every day. My life practice was to embrace family and professional obligations, not shirk them. When I received the hospital's call, I overreacted. Motivated by guilt, I turned my back on my responsibilities in Austin to escort Mom to her next life.

I've seen friends stand alone in emotional free fall after failed marriages, thankful I never had to live their grief. My marriage was stronger than me and more resilient than my wife. Our union was pliable: yielding to difficulty, but never breaking. Our marriage shattered when I remained beside my mother in the farming community where Mom and I were raised.

My mother died six months ago. Now, I sit on a curb in a parking area in Roanoke, Virginia in emotional free fall. I am lost, cloaked in harmful emotions, and influenced by bitter feelings. The home my family worked hard to nurture is a lifeless skeleton; someone else's treasure spread across different living space, lacking symmetry and continuity.

This is the unspoken reason I walk the Appalachian Trail. Tough times require strong measures for me to confront reality without blinders of engrained bias and learned behavior accumulated over a lifetime.

When this walk ends, footpaths will switch back to paved streets and traffic lights. How I live before family, friends, co-workers, and strangers will matter. Do I embrace life-freeing truths taught by Nature in the wilderness settings? Or return to white noise and chaos to bulldoze through my remaining life experiences?

Nature does not measure sojourners. Time measures the backcountry visitor. Time will gauge me.

Chapter Two
Roanoke Virginia

Buddy-Boy arrived at the Labrador Breeder Kennel in Normandy, Tennessee with an old soul on June 9, 2006. My family christened our pet, Simpson's Buddy-Boy, when we registered him with the American Kennel Club. He was the last of 12 litter mates living with his sire and dam when we responded to the advertisement posted in our local newspaper. Buddy-Boy was indifferent when hunters, ranchers, and young families with children turned up to hand-pick their pets. When a new master arrived, our puppy stood, yawned, stretched, and then wandered away. Our dog found a stick to gnaw while he watched his brothers and sisters secure new homes. Buddy-Boy was waiting for me.

Seven years have passed since I placed Simpson's Buddy-Boy in a small cardboard carton and drove him to his new home in Nashville, Tennessee. He is now my trusted, 105-pound white Labrador. Buddy goes wherever I go. He is my guardian, roommate, food sharer, and trusted hiking companion. When I lay down on my bed to rest, Buddy sleeps on the floor next to me on his own soft pallet. With my Labrador by my side, further security is unnecessary.

Today is September 9, 2013. Buddy and I relax on a raised curb, waiting for our ride to Catawba—a hamlet outside Roanoke, Virginia. The Catawba Trailhead is our gateway to the Appalachian National Scenic Trail.

Buddy looks strong in the pre-dawn light. He retrieved his Frisbee in Kansas snow last winter and on Mobile, Alabama's hot asphalt streets this summer. Buddy can carry his new backpack with ease. The pack I purchased for this trip feels the same as every backpack I throw over my shoulders for the first time: heavy and awkward.

I've completed the minimal steps needed to prepare to hike the Appalachian Trail. My pack is stuffed with equipment, clothing, and foodstuff to get through several days in the wilderness. I purchased a *'Thru-Hikers' Companion'* book and maps from the Appalachian Trail Conservancy to help guide our course. And yes, I secured a ride to a trailhead leading south on the Appalachian Trail.

My plan is straightforward: jump in feet first, figure out the logistics while we walk the passage, get in physical shape on the go, and then adjust along the way. A novice outdoorsman, influenced by a book or movie to chase this bucket list item, will probably fail starting out this way.

My backcountry experience will carry us until we get our bearings during the first two weeks. I served in the United States Army as a paratrooper with the 82d Airborne Division. I descended to the Grand Canyon floor one morning and then climbed back to the rim the same afternoon; hiked the Appalachian Trail inside North Carolina for a week; finished a six-day backpacking trip in the Alaska wilderness; backpacked in the Big South Fork National River and Recreation Area in Tennessee and devoted every vacation day possible dodging tourists while my wife and I explored the trails around Sedona, Arizona.

"How much trouble can we get into?" I question myself as Adam's truck headlights illuminate us. Adam is our advocate. He is a high-tech, minimalist thinker; a family man, a local physician, and an avid outdoorsman. Buddy and I will rely on Adam and his co-worker, Maye, to keep us equipped, re-supplied, and medically sound throughout our backcountry adventure. These people are kind and generous individuals who have contributed time and talent to get us to the Appalachian Trail, today.

Over the years, I've read outstanding books describing encounters in the wilderness and through the Appalachian Trail. My favorites are: *Wild*, by Cheryl Strayed, *A Walk in the Woods*, by Bill Bryson, and *AWOL on the Appalachian Trail* by David Miller. If these ordinary folks can survive the Pacific Crest Trail and Appalachian Trail to recount their narratives, Buddy and I will find a way.

"I will find a way," I repeat to myself, as I watch the windshield wipers scrape early morning mist from Adam's windshield. I recognize my dog and I are starting the most physical and emotional challenge of my life.

Self-confidence delivers Simpson's Buddy-Boy and me to the Catawba Trail Trailhead. Our hearts will decide whether we fulfill this dream. I am not a novice and I am not young. I am a 58-year-old man and Buddy is a seven-year-old dog. Between the two of us, we have zero experience completing a long-distance walk at this age, in this heat, in a drought, and in the wilderness by ourselves.

"Adam, what the hell was I thinking when I signed us up for this undertaking?" I announce, as reality's weight settles on my shoulders. "Buddy and I will pay a price for my failure to prepare for a journey of this magnitude," I acknowledge to my friend.

Adam smiles with confidence and pats my shoulder.

"You'll be fine, Jimmy Doug. Relax and drink your coffee. The trailhead parking area is a mile up this road."

Buddy rests with his backside on the bench seat in the back and places his block head next to my headrest. I reach up and lay my hand on the side of his face and wonder:

Can you understand my thoughts this morning, Sweet-Boy?

My hiking partner is calm and collected. He reaches over the front seat and licks my cheek. It's Buddy's way to say: *"Relax Poppy. We are free. Let's have fun."*

Trailheads exist at road junctions, parking lots, neighborhoods, and side trails. The Catawba Virginia Trailhead resides at a high traffic location. High traffic trailheads are easy to identify. They resemble small parks with trash cans, parking spaces, and a bulletin board packed with trail information.

Most trailheads include a wooden sign with carved letters, and a white blaze painted nearby. Wilderness signs are navigation tools, placed at strategic locations on the footpath. They provide hikers the name, distance, and direction to shelters or other landmarks. These guideposts are a source of encouragement or a cause for despair depending on remaining daylight hours, weather factors, hiker stamina, and walking distance.

I pay the price of missing the wilderness signs until I learn to concentrate on my surroundings. My biggest challenge is finding a sign when the footpath crosses a road surface or an open field. My mistake is assuming the dirt paths align when the route crosses open space. These trail intersections seldom fall in line. Sometimes, trail intersections are close. Other times, I walk a distance on a hard surface or a field of tall grass to rejoin the footpath. I've learned to plan for staggering exit and entrance points. This way, I'm less likely to experience the powerful 'lost in the woods' emotion.

When trails face each other, I'm happy. I cross the road and continue my trek. When they don't link-up, I relax and pay attention. A sign exists. I've had to remind myself more than once that the Appalachian Trail does not abandon its walkers in the middle of the woods. Search the tree line in both directions for the white blaze. White paint will occupy a tree, a rock, a stake driven in the ground, or a road surface.

The Catawba Trailhead sign stands beside a bulletin board between the parking area and the Appalachian Trail. When Buddy and I have our equipment on our backs and my poles are in my hands, we shake hands with Adam and walk past the wooden sign. Adam beams when we stop where the parking lot gravel meets the footpath dirt. We shift our pack weight and glance back to the life we know.

Reece was my wife for 32 years. She called this morning. Reese may not stand here with us now, but she is present. She was positive throughout our conversation, always expressing her best energy. As hard as she tried, she couldn't suppress her fear for our safety. Her forethought has merit. I should be apprehensive today, but I'm not. If personal safety is the standard, Buddy and I need to take our packs off and stay in this parking lot. I can't promise Reece we will be safe, but I pledge to be careful when I end our conversation.

It's dangerous to confuse wilderness encounters with romanticized fiction. Nature is unpredictable, and the backcountry is unforgiving when accidents occur. Hikers must exercise caution to survive well. How I manage risk will determine the condition Buddy and I will be in when we return to family and friends.

Twelve months have passed since I quit running rock-laden hills to prepare for today. I am eager to learn what the Appalachian Trail offers us. As I raise my hand and wave a 'goodbye for now' to Adam and Maye, I am reminded of my reality: I give up what I understand, to face the unknown by myself, for months.

"Not to worry," I reason out loud, smiling at Buddy. He grins back, and we start a walk I hope will last over 800 miles. It is a foot trip I propose we finish during the months of September through November 2013.

I take the lead and Buddy slips behind me with his nose a foot from the back of my left knee. Buddy's dog tags jingle in rhythm with the bear bell attached to my pack. Both instruments clatter in cadence with the nominal pace I want to sustain this morning. When we find a walking tempo, I describe to Buddy what I expect to share with nature on our wilderness journey.

"Buddy, you and I are now backcountry walkers hiking on the Appalachian Trail. We will walk under forest tree canopies, move across streams and creeks springing from hidden rocks embedded in sides of towering foothills, and search for the route when grass covers dirt paths in fields shared with grazing animals. We will persevere through painful strides as we invest in the chance to dance over rock-laden mountain ascents and descents, endure what comes our way each day for the opportunity to rest on summits, and enjoy the breeze crossing the ridgeline on this path called the 'Appalachian Trail'.

Buddy moves to my side when I finish speaking and my breathing settles. He nudges my leg in his playful way as if to say: *"I'm with you, Poppy."*

I reach down and stroke Buddy's head while we walk together.

"Yes, you are, Sweet-Boy. Let's have fun!"

Chapter Three
Catawba Creek

Mount Katahdin's Baxter Peak is the Appalachian Trail's northern terminus. Northbound thru-hikers typically start from the Appalachian Trail's southern terminus at Springer Mountain Georgia in early spring, so they can finish their 2,200-mile trek at Baxter Peak before Maine's winter begins in October. Since I start my backcountry walk at the tail end of the 2013 hiking season, I hope to backpack through half the Appalachian Trail this year, retire to Austin for the winter, and then complete my thru-hike at Baxter Peak during the normal 2014 hiking season.

Today's goal is Pickle Branch Shelter. Buddy and I plan to walk 12 miles our first day for the opportunity to sleep with a hard roof over our head. Within minutes of leaving Adam at the Catawba Trailhead, I confront an abrupt shift in topography and elevation.

I laugh aloud and shake my head from side-to-side in disbelief.

"So much for tracking a groomed path in a managed park setting, Buddy."

Buddy is a patient athlete. He waits for me to go up our first ascent. I pause to reposition my overloaded kit, then join one foot with the rising path. When I finish placing my lead foot on the incline, I set the other foot and push hard, advancing both feet up the sharp rise. The natural force required to complete this simple step is impressive.

The last time I felt this unprepared to face a physical challenge, I was a middle-aged, 254-pound man. I'd mounted my road bicycle for the first time in years and attempted to climb a small hill in Austin, Texas. I barely completed the ascent without dismounting and walking my bike to the hilltop. My body was sore for days after I returned the bicycle to its familiar hook in the garage.

Newcomers should seek guidance from a mentor when they undertake risk-based activities. It's more pleasant, less expensive, and less painful to learn from someone else's mistakes.

I regarded myself a mentor to new backpackers when I prepared for this trip. My backpack is loaded with quality equipment I culled from an assortment of gear I carried on other backcountry trips. I packed: food, water, extra shoes, lighters, a headlamp with extra batteries, a medical kit, a change of clothes with extra socks, raincoat and rain pants, a sleeping bag and air mattress, a ground cover, a tent, a cup, spoon and plastic bowl, a Swiss Army knife, a stove and fuel, water filtration equipment, cords and a rope, a pen and writing paper, maps, Ibuprofen, toilet paper, soap, a towel, deodorant, toothpaste with a toothbrush, and a leash. Based on the items I tote, I am a skilled backcountry walker. The way I struggle to walk up the grade wearing this loaded pack, I am a newcomer!

Backpack weight matters; the lighter the better. You can carry an overloaded pack to work out on residential streets, high school stadium bleachers, and small hills for an hour or two at a time, but don't try shouldering the same weight in the wilderness on a mountain's weather-beaten terrain. The summit experience will spoil your day and hurt your pocketbook when you drop quality supplies and equipment beside the wilderness trail for someone else to carry and use.

Adam and I discussed minimalist theory with sales people at each outfitter store we visited while preparing for this trip. I presumed I understood the minimalist approach to equipment weight: buy ultra-light equipment. I missed what "essential food and equipment" means carrying the weight of true life necessities on my back, day after day, ascending and descending mountains carved with rugged trails.

When I repacked my kit for the last time last night, I did not favor total weight or balance in the strategy. I will pay an enormous price for fitting volume in limited storage space.

I've ridden my bicycle to scale mountain passes and similar grade, on long, steep hills. The effort is formidable. This morning, this small hill requires the same grind with equal pain. I am embarrassed.

Buddy doesn't need words to express his thoughts.

"Poppy, why are you surprised you are sucking air on the first hill? The sum of your physical preparation for this journey was two or three brief runs this summer and tossing me Frisbees to chase in the Kansas snow and Alabaman heat."

"You're right, Buddy-Boy. I'm not prepared. Let's quit before I hurt myself."

"No way, Poppy. Let's go. We can rest walking downhill."

I pause again, midway through the steepest climb we've come upon this morning. My legs and shoulders need a break from my fight with an overloaded pack I can't balance, and the work required to negotiate this terrain.

I'm aware stopping my momentum on this harsh ascent may be problematic. I'm so tired that I still pause. When I reach across my torso and twist my hips to remove a water bottle from its pack sleeve, my legs buckle, and the bulky backpack pulls my feet out from under me. Before I can counter, I'm on the ground. My boots are above my head, and I plummet downhill until I tumble into my hiking partner. The full force of my fall takes Buddy's feet out, and we roll as a tangled mess to a level surface.

I lie still for a moment and then try to untangle from my backpack and pull myself together. Relief replaces fear when Buddy scrambles to his feet, shakes his equipment into place, and moves toward me with a regular stride.

I sink to my knees to stare Buddy straight in the eyes while I adjust his pack and remove vegetation from his coat. Buddy rewards me, leaning forward to deliver a lick to my cheek and rest his head on my shoulder. My dog is a strong animal and a sympathetic friend.

"Buddy, I'm sorry I'm not prepared to be here. I'm grateful you aren't hurt. We are both lucky I didn't need to call for rescue the first few hours on the trail."

Buddy smiles as I lovingly grab both his ears, return his grin, and pull his face toward me until we are nose-to-nose.

"Buddy, may I ask you a favor? Do you mind if we keep this mishap to ourselves?"

Buddy-Boy's eyes answer with a leader's truth.

"Poppy, I'm okay. Please shake off this accident. Today is the first day. Remember the plan. You will get in shape and figure

out what we need as we push forward. Don't quit. I need you and I am not going home until we finish."

We spend the morning hiking false flats with minor roller-coaster hills on the Catawba Mountain Ridgeline, until we drop 500 feet in elevation to Catawba Creek. This stream is a hidden treat available to anybody willing to walk south a few miles from Catawba Trailhead. We slow our pace to enjoy the approach to this treasure after our hectic start. A natural swimming hole has formed in a park setting at the bottom of the slope we descend.

As we near the pleasant scenery, I remind Buddy, "This creek is the setting we can expect each evening when we camp. We will rely on this abundant reserve of water to supply our water bottles for use on the trail and our cooking pot for dinner and breakfast meals. We will enjoy wading in these waters on humid days and soaking in them on balmy nights."

The knowledge I share with Buddy isn't derived from reading a map, studying my guidebook, or surveying weather reports. I make today's hydration plans based on the Appalachian Trail fantasy I considered for months in Kansas. My dog recognizes that I'm daydreaming and seizes his opportunity to revel in his own amusement. Buddy is water-bound in perfect stride.

"Buddy, come here. Please stop before your pack gets soaked," I shout, using my best dog-master tone.

My dog rejects my voice for the first time on our journey. He does not alter his pace or his path to the creek bank. Most importantly, he does not consider the equipment on his back when he stretches his body to full length and leaps for the water. He lands in the swimming hole, creating a colossal splash.

What can I do but laugh with delight for my Labrador? I won't scold Buddy and I can't resist watching him play. The water weight Buddy carries now will teach him to look after his backpack.

When Buddy-Boy drinks his fill and finishes frolicking in the clean, cool creek water, I remove his pack and dry myself. Buddy chases squirrels while I sit on the upper bank to rest and consider what might lie ahead for us today.

I carry two water bottles in their backpack sleeves when we arrive at this park setting. One bottle holds water filled from a kitchen sink in Roanoke, Virginia. The other container holds air. Before I hoist our kits onto our shoulders to leave this creek bank, I should drink the water I carry and refill both empty bottles. I refuse to complete this rudimentary step. Why go through all the trouble? I have a full bottle and I believe what I told Buddy: the Appalachian Trail is rich with water resources.

Adam touched on the topic of Central Virginia drought during our conversations. His brief comments never registered with me as I drank coffee from Starbucks and "Route 44" Diet Cherry Limeades from Sonic. We focused on filtration systems and the best way to transport water. Adam prefers to carry a camelback with an integrated filtration system stored in his backpack. My habit is water bottles. I favor iodine tablets to purify water when I am hiking.

The Army trained me to use iodine to create safe drinking water 40 years ago. It's a simple procedure: open the protective package, drop in the tablets, shake the container, wait four hours, and then drink the water. I'm confident using iodine tablets for short periods of time. Tablets are efficient, lightweight, and easy to manage on the move. I worry ingesting iodine every day for two months may create unforeseen complications. Adam was supportive when I shared my concern. He helped me choose top-line water filtration equipment at an outfitter in Salem, Virginia.

In my haste to get on the Appalachian Trail, I neglected to practice using the filtration equipment, let alone read the instructions. Given my physical effort this morning, both bottles should be empty. I drank one bottle; I need to hydrate my body, and I'm walking away from this source of cool, clean, running water.

"Not a problem, the Appalachian Trail has plenty of water," I remind myself. *"Buddy will drink from streams, today. I will manage the water in my second bottle until we arrive at our campsite. The shelter is eight miles away, little more than a 10K run; three hours walking time. I will boil water for the next day when we camp tonight. We can try out the water filtration equipment tomorrow when we stop for lunch."*

I describe my plan to Buddy without acknowledging my hiking partner's feedback.

"Poppy, you know what is necessary to sustain endurance effort. You consumed large amounts of water every day at work and home, preparing to ride or run. I don't understand. Why aren't you drinking water this morning? I swam to cool-off and

drank till I wanted to heave. Be smart, Poppy. Drink. I depend on you."

Buddy and I are good at making our thoughts known to each other without speaking. I'm sorry I missed this advice.

We finish our first four miles when we walk across the elevated footbridge covering Catawba Creek. Two college students from Virginia Tech University sit on the bank of this narrowing band of water, treating blisters and filling every water container they carry.

I pause and extend a friendly greeting.

"Hey guys. An ideal pool of water waits for you a mile up the trail."

Both young men smile, say "thanks", and keep filling their bottles and hydration reservoirs.

I'm a city boy; fresh from a parking lot near Roanoke, Virginia. My senses have not adjusted to wilderness awareness. As a newcomer, I neglect the warning the scene below conveys: Jimmy Doug, you, and your dog face tough terrain with no water in sight.

The young man tending the cook stove stops his work to speak directly to me.

"We laid eyes on 'Dragon's Tooth' before we descended Cove Mountain a few miles back. The descent is by far the toughest topography we've experienced on this part of the Appalachian Trail."

The other young man working his water purification apparatus glances up and adds:

"I cannot imagine how you will climb Dragon's Tooth with your dog, sir. Good luck!" he declares, as he smiles and returns his attention to filling his hydration reservoir.

I wave and move on without reacting. When Buddy and I are out of earshot, I stop to adjust my dog's pack and pat his head.

"Don't worry, Pal. This is Virginia. These men have never seen a Tennessee-bred, Texas-raised Labrador. You are an athlete: clever, strong, and agile. We'll summit Cove Mountain and view Dragon's Tooth this afternoon."

Buddy's not concerned. He wags his tail and sets out on the dirt path before I can take the lead. We spend the rest of the morning hiking through woods on bottom land; negotiating fence ladders I climb over and Buddy crawls underneath to reach new ground. The sky is overcast, and the temperature is cool with low humidity. We walk across grass fields that hikers share with private land owners and walk past field animals the ranchers manage. Buddy continues to hydrate himself at water crossings whenever he chooses. This is the Appalachian National Scenic Trail I expected when I sat with Mom in Kansas.

Chapter Four
Dragon's Tooth

White splotches painted on tree trunks and a worn footpath guide us from the open countryside, fresh air, spacious sky, and streaming water to the backcountry's doorstep.

Six miles into today's walk we cross VA624 and advance onto mountains that stand below the Jefferson National Forest's tree canopy.

The forest wraps visitors in a natural cocoon of promising greens and decaying browns, mixed in filtered sunlight. The atmosphere is eerie. I move in solitude—aware I do not walk alone. I sense the spirit of those who traversed this land before my time. Buddy and I pierce the veil separating the land of the living and wilderness unknown with nowhere to hide.

Are you afraid in the dark? Best stay home unless you walk the wilderness trails with your companions. The Appalachian Trail does not accommodate visitors intimidated by the unknown. Night lights do not illuminate what imaginations create in these strange surroundings. I accept my hair will stand on end in fear, from time-to-time, as I confront the undefined for the chance to pass through this surreal environment.

I have jumped from aircraft for the U.S. Army. Life under Jefferson National Forest's tree canopy reminds me when I parachuted from those flying machines to float between heaven and earth:

Sit recalling the good times.
Contemplate the unknown.
Stand up.
Stretch your muscles.
Check your equipment.
Hook up.
Press forward.

Shuffle to the door.
Fill the exit.
Watch ground race shadows.
See the green light.
Listen for the go signal.
Brace and leap.
Fall fast.
Count to four.
Wait in suspense.
Trust what can't be controlled.
Straps pull hard.
Cords snap taunt.
Glance up and express your gratitude.
Float below a full canopy.
Stand above the rising earth.
Discover silence.
Sense nature's voice encase and penetrate.
Accept the surreal aware reality rushes to close the gap.
Pick a soft-landing spot.
Manage what fights direction.
Embrace what is given.
Land with grace; dignity may not be a choice.
Check your equipment.
Move forward to survive.

Each day I contemplated the unknown and jumped, my faith was honored. Today, my spirit soars as I hike Cove Mountain under the Jefferson National Forest's tree canopy. Buddy and I glide across grades that produce pain this morning. Switchbacks help. A switchback is a sharp curve in the route that cuts against a steep mountainside. Switchbacks allow a passerby to zigzag across a mountainside at reasonable grades to avoid climbing straight up or straight down a harsh grade.

Once our pace becomes routine, I daydream. Buddy nuzzles my hand to wake me from deep thought when Cove Mountain's undulating footpath transforms into an expansive clearing. This opening must be a primitive campsite. There are no campers present, but I recognize where the tents stood, and campfires provided energy to heat water and produce warmth.

I smile, tilt my ball cap away from my forehead, wipe my brow, and then reach for my map while I glance toward my forgotten hiking partner.

"Hello Buddy-Boy. Is mountain climbing as fun as playing in stream crossings? Are you enjoying the forest canopy and the switchbacks?"

Buddy's brown eyes glisten. It's his way to say, *"It's all fun, Poppy."*

"Do you see the wooden sign?" I ask, pointing to a landmark standing at the clearing's far-right edge. "This must be the junction where the Appalachian Trail merges with the Boy Scout Connector Trail. Two more miles and we arrive at the Dragon's Tooth Trailhead."

Buddy wags his tail. He brushes the full length of his body against my leg, swings around, and waits for me to adjust his kit and scratch his back. My friend is hydrated and content. Buddy spent the morning walking on grass and playing in water. I'm thirsty. Logic tells me people camp near active water sources. I scan the campground for a blue painted symbol designating the route that would lead us to water.

I don't see blue paint, but I recognize a rocky creek bed at the far end of the clearing.

"Look, Buddy," I say, pointing toward the rocks. "Water may run in those pockets."

Buddy isn't interested in the creek bed. My Labrador has something else on his mind. He reaches with his left paw and grazes the side of my leg to gain my attention.

"Poppy, let's be wise. We've walked for several hours and covered six miles. You're looking rough. We've enjoyed a good first day. Let's stop here and get organized for tomorrow's ascent to Dragon's Tooth. I want to show the Virginia Tech students how a big dog handles a tough mountain pass. What do you say, Poppy?"

"Good thought, Sweet-Boy. Let's focus on finding water to drink, then we can relax. Let's check out the creek bed. We will camp here if we find water to cook with and drink."

Buddy doesn't wait for my command. When my dog walks across the rocks without lowering his head, my mind-set shifts from thirsty to parched. *No water.* The drought Adam mentioned must be more acute than I imagined.

I decide the best approach is to walk for water.

"Let's go, Buddy-Boy," I say, attempting to sound hopeful for my hiking partner. "We will find water up ahead. In the meantime, let's be careful managing the fluid we have left in this bottle."

I remove the water bottle cap, fill it, and give Buddy his first ration. My dog licks every drop from the container's lid.

The topography leading from the campsite is kind. I'm grateful for the reprieve. Buddy-Boy and I cannot support high exertion levels on this ration for long.

"I guess the college boys were having a crummy morning, Buddy. This grade is different, but not overpowering."

Buddy agrees. He is confident. He trots around me, takes the lead, and serves as path finder whenever the spirit moves him. I lose sight of Buddy as I surrender to another daydream. When the footpath bends then straightens, I spot him sitting on the trail, facing a rock wall.

"Buddy, why have you halted? What do you see? Are you hurt, Big-Boy?"

My Labrador looks at me without altering his posture as if to say, *"Poppy, come look at this wall. This obstacle is the Appalachian Trail passageway."*

I study the rock wall and agree with my hiking partner.

"You are right, Buddy-Boy. Those are white blazes painted on the rock's surface."

Buddy's position is now my position. We both stare toward the sky, standing before this hindrance with hushed respect. The wall rises higher than my line of sight. Based on the climbing surface I can see; Buddy and I do not belong here. It's a waste of time to contemplate the series of walls we can't see, yet we must confront to summit Cove Mountain.

I hope Buddy has an answer for this challenge. Based on my assessment, I doubt my skill to scale this wall wearing heavy hiking boots and carrying a 50-pound pack. The college students were correct to question how Buddy would ascend this rock monster. I can't tote him.

Buddy and I select a course of action fitting our predicament. We sit side by side on the dirt path and share a snack bar I pull from my pants' side pocket. When we finish eating, I consider Buddy-Boy's disposition. He's content and confident. He smiles and hangs his tongue from his mouth to one side. His heart rate is regular, and he is ready to play.

"Buddy, can we scale this mountain pass? We can hike back to the trailhead serving the Boy Scout Campsite if this ascent is too technical. There is no reason to risk a serious fall. When we find a ride, we'll start anew someplace else."

Buddy looks me straight in the eyes and then licks me right on the mouth. It's his way of telling me, *"Stop this nonsense, Poppy. Get moving."*

I'm not ready to change position. I continue to sit with my climbing partner at the base of this challenge, in deep thought. Adam and the salesman at the Outfitter in Salem, Virginia discussed this natural obstacle. I don't remember them specifically say 'Dragon's Tooth', but this must be it. The advance to the Dragon's Tooth spur trail is a 0.7-mile ascent filled with a series of severe rock grade that can take day-hikers wearing daypacks hours to climb. There is no water at the summit.

When the salesman spoke of Dragon's Tooth, he directed his words toward Adam, but looked at Buddy and then at me and said:

"Adam, do you remember steel rebar drilled into the rock face at various wall sections? Those hand grips make an extreme grade accessible for the average hiker. I use those ladders every time I climb the mountain pass to Dragon's Tooth."

The salesman returned to his discourse with us when Adam confirmed his assessment.

"Do you have a dog?" the merchant asked Adam without waiting for a response. "My pet is short in stature and is agile. I doubt she can handle Dragon's Tooth at the steepest grades. Although, we've never tried. She's strong and athletic, but this climb is extreme for a pet. My dog gets upset with me, but I leave her home when I climb Cove Mountain to Dragon's Tooth."

True to the Appalachian Trail spirit, the outfitter shared information without offering an opinion whether Buddy and I can carry out this task, alone or together.

I am grateful I lacked personal knowledge to grasp what the outfitter had outlined for me. If I had the knowledge, I'd save this challenge for another day. I reach over and rub Buddy's head when I complete this cautious, but unfair judgment.

"I'm glad we are here, Buddy. We will work together to scale this wall."

In my past, I've concentrated on a complex fix and missed a simple solution to a complicated problem. Maybe we missed an alternate route today. Only one way to find out. We walk south, tracing the wall's face to its end without discovering a different path. When we return to the white blazes painted in ascending order, we retrace the steps that led us to the wall. When I conclude my investigation, we still stare at white blazes painted on the rock. My 105 pound Labrador and I cannot avoid this skills test. This rock face is the passageway to Cove Mountain's summit, the spur trail to Dragon's Tooth, and the southbound Appalachian Trail.

If I could send my pack to the top of Cove Mountain by elevator or pulley with Buddy in tow, I'd still question my ability to ascend this mountain pass. I accept risk when I manage uncertainty in a structured environment, and I depend on proven knowledge. I'm not confident wearing heavy boots and carrying a loaded backpack I fell with this morning. This wall demands I step-up and face danger, depending on my abilities that have yet to be tested.

The challenge today is ignoring fear and taking the first step when a safe passage isn't discernible. Buddy and I have two choices: be cautious and leave, or accept this ultimatum. I resolve to climb up to the Appalachian Trail at Cove Mountain and extend our journey. Adrenaline will carry us through this unknown environment. We may not summit Cove Mountain and view Dragon's Tooth today, but it won't be from the lack of trying.

Staring at this hindrance, I'm reminded of a different time. My daughter and I dealt with a similar challenge backpacking in Alaska.

"What are you contemplating, Daddy?"

"Honey, I'm sifting through your confrontation with the Alaskan moose. You left an impression, Lacey. People do not charge moose. You ran across Lake Bennett's shore line, camera in hand, hollering at a damn moose to stop and come back for a picture. The creature never turned back when he got an eyeful of you coming his way. Must have been the clothes you were wearing: florescent pink racing tights and clogs, and an orange jacket with a matching stocking cap," I answer, offering a proud father's smile.

"I'm disappointed we're leaving in 30 minutes. I'd love to watch someone else test your outfit with a bear. If your apparel runs off the bear the same as the moose, the family will strike gold marketing, 'Lacey's Backcountry Clothing and Equipment'."

"Oh, Daddy, stop it," Lacey laughs with me, and then gives me a hug. "I know you and your story telling. I'm sure I'll hear this narrative, again. When and where—the possibilities are endless."

Lacey and I appreciate our last minutes in the Alaskan wilderness. We walk and talk outside the remote train station in Bennett, British Columbia, relishing Lake Bennett's picturesque backdrop. Our train services the White Pass and Yukon Route. We created a lifetime memory in this backcountry. Lacey and I hiked the Chilkoot Trail, a 33-mile footpath, passing through the Coast Mountains. Our ride will arrive in a few minutes to return us to our origination point: Skagway, Alaska. The time has arrived to return home and re-engage in life.

A day will come when age forces me to enjoy panoramic views of striking shorelines, blue glaciers, and jumping whales from a ship's railing. That's okay. I'll drink wine, smoke cigars, and wait for the ship to dock in Skagway, Alaska. When I leave the vessel, I'll stroll to restaurants I favor to eat marvelous seafood served by the locals. I swear kitchen staff sticks a fishing pole out their kitchen windows to catch the fish I order.

When I'm filled with oysters, shrimp, crab, white bass, salmon, and Alaskan beer, I'll board this train again to cherish my next excursion into this backcountry. The details of this Chilkoot Trail experience will leap to life watching the wilderness' outer rim skirt past my passenger car window. A train ride in the Alaska frontier will be enough to feed my soul.

Today, I'm thankful for the gift to devote six days to my daughter. I appreciate Lacey's choice for this trip. I'm happiest when I carry a backpack and climb elevations delivering glacier water from fast-moving streams. Hard climbs are worth the effort to witness nature transform with changing altitude.

Lacey and I climbed Chilkoot Pass two days ago in the chilling fog. The experience was life altering. The word 'climb' is misstating action. We crawled with fingers, knees, and toes more than we stood inside a wet cloud blanketing the mountain pass. We moved up and over slick, Volkswagen Beetle-sized boulders to cross the Canadian border. I may forget my route home one day. I will always remember working my way up those boulders between my companions, Leah and Melissa, confident my daughter and her friend, Jennie, were safe 10 yards back. We operated as a unit, confronting our fears together and pushing up the pass through the cloud cover as a team.

I'm a mature man. I stay quiet when I'm surrounded by a sister on each side and two best friends stationed below my feet. Our party was confident in their surroundings when I heard four voices in perpetual conversation. I spoke to my climbing partners when I could hear my breathing and sense apprehension turn into fear. I hoped a calm voice could break the spell with an encouraging word and a distracting comment.

"Chilkoot Pass is a splendid test for us in this weather," are calming words I offered my companions. "Did the professor inform you this risk was present when he selected this location for our trip?"

"No way we knew," the sisters chime in together.

"I doubt the professor was aware this risk existed. No one could predict this fog. I'm delighted I'm here, but I'm grateful Lacey's mother can't see what we are doing. I can't believe I brought my daughter up this pass."

A rock the size of a bowling ball skipped by Melissa a few minutes later. I couldn't act to help Lacey or Jenny. Fate would be their friend I realized while I watched the rock bounce downhill. The rock sailed right over Lacey's and Jenny's heads. The girls survived unscathed, this time.

For me, living with calculated risk is the thrill of the struggle. One moment, I surrender potential life. The next moment, existence continues with a racing heartbeat, shortness of breath, and a new respect for surroundings. I choose this hobby for me. Lacey chose this risk for us when she encouraged her favorite law school professor to plan this summer trip. I'm glad she did.

When we finished the ascent, Lacey displayed symptoms of hypothermia. A warming hut awaited us when we reached the top of Chilkoot Pass. Young couples filled the small room, huddling together to stay warm. These strangers offered Lacey the best remedies available: hard liquor from flasks and a warm coat belonging to a man who took it off his back. These backcountry adventurists taught me to expect unexpected acts of kindness from generous strangers asking nothing in return in a wilderness setting.

"Daddy, you understand this trip may be the last vacation we will share by ourselves, right? Priorities and time commitments are shifting. I'm a wife now. I will be a mother one day. Baylor Law School courses are demanding. When I conclude my classes next year, I add career and student loan payments to my blend of new life priorities."

"Right," I answered. Why does this one-word affirmation cause grief? It's simple: it is because I'm not prepared to embrace her new life priorities for myself. Raising my children for two decades with their mother has been an irreplaceable gift. Now, it's my time to turn over this precious blessing to another man, and the family he and my daughter create.

"I understand, Honey. Your mother and I raised a remarkable young adult. We will enjoy watching you flourish as a couple and family. You two will impact the lives of everyone you touch going forward. I appreciate our time here. We've created another lifetime memory."

Reece is a wise woman. When Lacey was a newborn, Reece sat in my lap with Lacey in her arms.

"Honey, your daughter will come to share your lap. Accept the gift when she gives it. You will be her safe place when she needs assurance. Love her, listen to her without judgment, and help her realize she is lovely; inside and out. Receive her kisses and hold her close when she hugs you. Love your daughter without limitation and she will always come to you. Prepare your daughter to make the best choice when she picks her husband. She will recognize her future-husband, observing how you treat her right here in your arms."

I burned this wisdom into my spirit with the same conviction I said "I do", the night I married my daughter's mother. I lived out this vow before Lacey to its positive end. Her commitment to herself, her husband, and her family is unbreakable.

"What's next for you, Daddy?" Lacey asks after we sit in silence for a time.

"Well, let's see. I finished the 200-mile Seattle to Portland one-day bike event in less than 10 hours before this trip. That event ends my bicycling challenges. I want to hike the Grand Canyon's South Kaibab Trail from top to bottom and back in one day. I hope to run a Boston Qualifying Marathon before I walk the entire Appalachian Trail. When I complete this list of 'what's next', I will be content writing stories and savoring 'whatever is next' for my children and grandchildren."

Buddy drags his sharp claws against my shirtsleeve and barks, forcing me to return to the task at hand.

"Poppy, quit stalling. Let's go."

"You're right, Buddy. We can scale this wall. I'm prepared to start when you are ready. If Lacey and I can climb Chilkoot Pass, wearing these boots, with our friends, in fog on slick rock, we'll discover the way to summit Cove Mountain."

My hiking companion doesn't hesitate. He moves past me to sit at a spot he's selected to start the climb. When Buddy turns his head, I accept the place he designates. We smile, and I step up to begin my ascent. I depend on my hands and feet to balance on a thin ledge, hopeful my dog will follow me up the path I blaze for him. I do not pause until I reach the first plateau and consider the next challenging wall.

On to Plan B: Buddy hasn't moved his butt. He still wears his magnificent smile. I lay my equipment on the rock floor dividing the walls, descend half the rock wall I scaled, and signal for my dog to "come". Buddy looks at me and whimpers, then barks and paces back and forth across the ground without advancing up the rock.

On to Plan C: I return to the ground and take Buddy's pack off, hoping this will inspire him to try on his own. I move up the rock carrying his gear in one hand and ascend with my other hand. This is a risk I accept; to hike with my Labrador. I encourage Buddy to follow me as I go. When I get to the top, my companion is barking at me from the ground. My dog is cheering for me. Given his station, Buddy-Boy must think rock climbing is a spectator sport.

On to Plan D: I leave Buddy's pack beside my equipment and descend to the ground, again. This time, I have a serious conversation with my beloved friend and hiking companion.

"Buddy, I cannot carry you up this mountain pass. You can scale these walls. If you refuse to climb, I am going back for our equipment and I am taking you home."

My plan is to push Buddy until he climbs on his own. I realize my idea is ridiculous, but desperate times call for compelling measures, right? Before I can step behind Buddy, he returns to the place he sat when I arrived at the rock wall and scales the obstacle without delay. I stand on the ground watching with awe-filled respect. Buddy's effort is courage in motion. His achievement may be the finest athletic performance I've witnessed in person.

Buddy executes his plan to get me to the top of Cove Mountain. At each section, he makes me repeat the same steps: I climb with my backpack, return for Buddy's pack, and sometimes return to encourage Buddy before he scales the wall. I never know why he makes me go through this ritual before he takes his turn. He does not have a problem completing this climb.

We finish the 0.7-mile challenge in just under four hours. I navigate many wall sections several times before we summit Cove Mountain. The outfitter in Salem Virginia was right. I use rebar ladders to scale walls at the pass' steepest points. Buddy finds his own way.

"Buddy-Boy, you were magnificent this afternoon. I wish the Virginia Tech gentlemen climbed with us. You showed me how a big dog ascends this mountain pass. I hope you are pleased. I'm proud of you, Sweet-Boy. Shall we visit Dragon's Tooth?" I ask when we see signage advertising the footpath to Dragon's Tooth.

Buddy responds by extending his front legs, resting on his haunches, and laying his belly on the dirt. We agree. Buddy and I rest beside the Dragon's Tooth Spur Trail Marker, nurse the water bottle level to six ounces, and share a dry supper.

I'm thankful Cove Mountain is merciful to her southbound visitors. We reap the climb's reward when we return to the footpath. The mountain provides miles of ridgeline to walk in the shade of her tree canopy. We fight dehydration and exhaustion without being exposed to hard inclines and declines or the full heat of the day. When the ridgeline ends, and the descent begins, my body and my mind yield to fluid depravation I contend with every marathon I run. I move with the flow of the terrain by sheer will; asleep on my feet more than awake as our route swings into a series of tight switchbacks I am hopeful will deliver us to the Pickle Branch Shelter.

I sense trouble when I hear Buddy muffle an abrupt bark and then see him rush forward to block our route. Adrenaline fails to mask fear when my protector sits alert and delivers a low guttural growl. My mind clears and my body fine tunes when Buddy erupts with a menacing growl I've never heard him project.

I witness the threat my dog perceives. A large animal has moved away from dense vegetation to shut off our path. A black bear stands watching us with four paws firmly implanted on the Appalachian Trail.

We have nowhere to run. A steep ravine falls to our left and a harsh incline stands to our right. I'm not sure how to react. Ringing Lacey's bear bell isn't a choice. I understand bear spray can be effective if you have the foresight to carry a canister. Unfortunately, I left my last spray can at the Juneau Alaska Airport. The large hunting knife I carry in Buddy's pack might be helpful if I can grab it before the bear attacks. I'll never know. Buddy doesn't grant me the chance to defend him.

This is my Labrador's fight. Simpson's Buddy-Boy leans forward in his sitting position and delivers one harsh snarl and a deep-throated bark. The black bear stares at Buddy without advancing or producing a sound. Buddy does not flinch. Uncounted seconds pass, and the bear relaxes. I fear the animal's next step. Fortunately, the beast elects to abandon our passageway and crash through the vegetation at a full run. The beast propels its body to the valley floor in a matter of moments, plunging down a grade I will soon traverse for a time on steep switchbacks to reach the bottom.

I understand I attended this extraordinary incident, but my psyche isn't ready to accept what my eyes have observed. What a spectacular moment in nature. The bear faced Buddy in its natural habitat and Buddy put his life on the line to protect me. I wish I could describe for you the emotion, the power, the athleticism, the courage, the energy, and the decision-making skills I absorbed on this wilderness footpath. But I can't. I am grateful I devoted the time and energy to experience this event for myself.

I am proud of Buddy, and thankful the bear graciously shares the forest with us today. As I contemplate these good thoughts, I realize the black-furred beast is heading toward the location Buddy and I will eat and sleep tonight.

"Perfect. We will finish our trek from Catawba to the Pickle Branch Shelter this evening, so that the bear can devour us for supper in comfort. Bear dinner. Nice thought, Jimmy Doug," I laugh to myself.

The switchbacks deposit us on level ground that transforms into head high weeds. The trail is difficult to see, so I follow the shortest and thinnest wall of plant life to its natural end. My guess is the correct choice. When we exit the foliage, we stand in a small meadow with an open view of the sky. We lose the pathway in the tall grass, but it's easy to see from this vantage point where the trail continues into the woods at the tree line.

"Buddy, I'm sure we are less than a mile from the shelter. As promised, we stand in an open space. Do we continue walking for water or stop to drink and eat?"

If I examine a map, Buddy might have a different answer. Since my map sits in his pack compartment, Buddy isn't willing to bet on my one-mile guess. He doesn't wait for me to remove his kit. He finds a soft patch of tall grass and stretches out to relax. Buddy has 'bonked'. In fact, we have both 'bonked'.

I take Buddy's pack off and rub his tired muscles before I remove my equipment and prop it beside my friend. We share the last of our water and a handful of jerky. Buddy falls asleep with his paw on my leg and me caressing his head.

I pass out with the sun shining above the tree line. I wake up, chilled and disoriented, with bright stars piercing the dark sky. When my eyes adjust, I see Buddy's silhouette in the distance. He's on point, guarding our perimeter.

"I wonder what he senses," I ask myself without wanting to know the answer.

Buddy trots toward me when I move my stiff body to a position I can rise from the ground. He arrives by my side before I stand and studies me with eyes saying: *"What's the plan Poppy? It's dark. I am hungry and thirsty, and we have neighbors walking in the woods. What should we do?"*

"Good question," I respond aloud, as I unzip the side pocket of my backpack to secure the headlamp I carried in Alaska. When I press the switch, the lamp works. When I secure the headlamp's elastic strap to my ball cap, the beam still produces light.

"That is a good start," I tell Buddy, as I open my kit to retrieve equipment I will need to stay warm and sleep on the ground.

I change the headlamp angle after I secure my rain jacket and set out my bedroll. When I touch the lightbulb enclosure, the plastic case's locking mechanism releases and the batteries spill to the ground.

Light vanishes with my night vision. We now stand together in the meadow in total darkness. I lose my composure for the first time today.

"Buddy, I can't set up my tent or feed you without light," I say with a tone that communicates an unnecessary sense of urgency.

Clear-minded people unzip their backpack side pocket. They calmly remove their cell phone, turn on the power, activate the flashlight application, find the batteries, and then fix their headlamp. Better yet, smart people forget the headlamp batteries tonight and use the flashlight to create a makeshift camp. Not me. I secure my lighter from a side pocket and flick it enough times to find one battery. I give up locating the second battery when I throw the lighter on the ground after the heat generated by the flame burns my fingers.

When my vision adapts to the dark, I place my sleeping bag and equipment on the ground cover and toss the tent on top to protect myself against the moisture and to offer another layer of warmth.

"What a day, Sweet-Boy. Your performance was exceptional. I hope you had fun. I did. Come here and make yourself comfortable," I whisper, as I close my sleeping bag around me to conclude day one. Buddy slides half his body under the tent and rests his head next to mine. I'm sound asleep before my eyelids firmly close.

Chapter Five
Pickle Branch Shelter

Last night, the expensive, self-inflating air mattress I carried for comfort in Alaska, Tennessee and North Carolina turned into a worthless, self-deflating ground cover. I don't care if I wake before dawn from a deep sleep on hard ground. We survived yesterday to relax this morning at Miller Cove between Cove Mountain and Brush Mountain. We scaled a difficult mountain pass and confronted a mature black bear without incident. As relevant, we slept without entertaining a furry visitor. *Thank you, Sweet-Buddy-Boy.*

Buddy is content, roaming the perimeter before daybreak. Why disturb my Labrador's fun when the sky is still thick with stars that vary in size and brightness? No reason exists from my vantage point, so I lay still and touch the gates to heaven with my eyes.

Buddy arrives by my side when sunlight peaks over the trees bordering the clearing. My dog delights in pestering me. He doesn't stop nudging me with his head until I make moves resembling an old man, beaten with a baseball bat, attempting to rise from the ground.

"Buddy, are you teasing me? You want to play? Respect your elder, puppy. I'm suffering a Dragon's Tooth hangover," I say with a grin, giving my pal a hug.

Buddy returns my smile when I finish scratching his back. My dog's thoughts are obvious.

"No excuses, Poppy. Let's go. I want my breakfast!"

"Come here, Buddy. You need to see this," I announce when I dismantle my sleeping pad. It turns out, the small stone I slept on last night is the missing headlamp battery. Buddy noses the object until he can mouth it, then he drops the troublemaker into my hand. When I place both batteries in their enclosure, I make sure I fasten the cover, and then drop my headlamp into a pack side pocket.

When I return my camping equipment to my backpack, I shift my attention to Buddy. His body is free of hot spots and his footpads are acceptable. I tip my ball cap to chasing Frisbees in Kansas snow and on Alabaman asphalt.

Buddy accepts his pack without argument. I slip his head through the harness, then manipulate the straps through his front legs to snap under his girth. When my equipment weight has settled onto my hips, we walk to the tree line and step back onto the trail leading us to water at Pickle Branch Shelter. A sign stands beside our footpath a tenth mile from where we fell asleep last night. A craftsman has carved "Pickle Branch Shelter" and a "left turn" arrow into the wood surface.

"Are you kidding me?" I chastise myself, exasperated with my poor woodsman skills. My decision to stop our hike without determining our location is the same as me sprawling on the street pavement and quitting a marathon a 0.10-mile from a finish line; maximum effort, no comfort, and no reward.

The arrow points left, so we turn left onto the Pickle Branch Shelter Side Trail and shuffle along a pleasant grade for 0.21 miles to arrive at the forest dwelling. Buddy heads for water when I remove his pack. I set our packs on the picnic table that stands in front of the small shelter and follow my Labrador to fill my water bottles for the first time since I turned the kitchen faucet off in Roanoke.

I enjoy watching as Buddy drinks from running water; lining parts of the empty creek bed before I break out the water filtration gear and read the instructions. Buddy knows I struggle when I'm required to follow written directions. We are both surprised when the parts fit together, and the device is easy to use.

Buddy lies on the opposite bank and watches with great interest as I draw water into the first bottle. My biggest problem this morning is getting the flat filter to stay seated in shallow stream pockets. The side used to harvest liquid keeps flipping over in the thin layer of water. Patience is the solution. When the bottle is full, I replace the top and fill the second container. I consume three receptacles at the stream and then filter water for two bottles to drink on the way to our next destination: Trout Creek.

Buddy is sound asleep when I finish filtering the fifth water bottle and fill my cook pot with creek water to boil at the picnic table.

"Wake up, Sweet-Boy. Let's go back to the shelter and eat breakfast."

Buddy carries two-cup servings of dry dog food, treats, a collapsible food bowl, a large water container, medical supplies, and a big hunting knife in his pack. We reduce his pack weight this morning, securing two dog food servings.

The picnic table top is a good cooking platform and a welcome seat. I'm pleased my stove still works as advertised. Creek water boils before I finish a pop tart. Buddy enjoys his pastry while I prepare a hot breakfast of coffee, oatmeal, and ramen noodles. I eat my meal with my feet sitting on the bench seat and my forearms resting on my thighs.

This is the first wilderness breakfast I've eaten in isolation. My spirit releases lifetime memories sharing packaged meals in nature with family, friends, and military mates. Reece stands out this morning. I recall her moving around similar campsites we shared at the Big South Fork National River and Recreation Area.

"Reece, where are you?" I asked, waking beside an empty sleeping bag after sharing a delicious night sleeping with my wife.

"I'm out here, Jimmy Doug. Your coffee is ready. Dress warm; the temperature is chilly this morning."

My wife worked hard in dawn's early light. When I unzipped the tent flap, Reece was standing by a cheerful fire she resurrected from the previous night's embers.

"Honey, you are amazing. I wish you'd waited for me to help."

"My treat, Jimmy Doug. Here is your coffee mixed with sweetener and hot chocolate. Breakfast water is boiling. I hope you're impressed with my campsite skills. I appreciate how much you respect your other backpacking companions."

My wife viewed our personal relationship from a unique perspective. Why did Reece believe she competed with anyone? She was my heart. I'm grateful she had chosen me to wake next to each morning and rest beside each night. Why did my wife believe she needed to impress me to earn my praise, approval, or acceptance?

My heart sinks and my mind is sad with the reminder my wife no longer shares my life.

"Buddy, I miss Nanny. I wish she was sitting beside me at Pickle Branch sipping hot coffee, watching you eat, and giving me grief for quitting before we reached the shelter yesterday. Did you know I invited Nanny to backpack the Appalachian Trail with us? I hoped we could share the wilderness experience to reconstruct the life you know we threw away."

Buddy is a big fan of pastries mixed with dry dog food. He's going right through his breakfast when he lifts his head and passes on an inquisitive glance.

"Poppy, why isn't Nanny here with us? Was she afraid?"

"No, Sweet-Boy. Nanny is strong, and she is in excellent physical condition. Her heart sympathized with my suggestion, but her mind wasn't prepared to let go of the enormous pain she and I created."

"I don't understand, Poppy. I've lived every day with you since we left Texas for Kansas. You love Nanny more than me."

"I understand, Buddy-Boy. Love cannot always overcome catastrophic disappointment. Sweet-Boy, you may not comprehend the reason I sit by myself this morning at Pickle Branch Shelter, but I recognize why Nanny has such contempt for me. Marriage partners preserve and protect. A spouse is attentive and mindful to honor their mate before others. Covenant maker's do not judge or demean, do not take a lover for granted, and do not detach emotionally or spiritually from a life-companion to walk alone.

"A woman's confidence should soar when her man looks her way, touches her skin, and speaks of her to others. Husbands are a wife's safe harbor when she is vulnerable or unsettled. He patiently supports his life-mate, listening intently while she expresses opinions or releases painful disappointment, without intolerance or judgment. A man waits for his spouse to reveal why she is insecure before he reacts poorly when she withholds love. Right, wrong, tired, distracted, busy, or with other commitments, a married man greets his wife, without excuse; where she stands with open arms and a tender heart.

"Buddy, I failed Nanny as a man, at a basic level. A husband never takes his eyes off the prize—his bride. A married man loves his wife. He takes pleasure in her, adores her, values her opinions, and respects her decisions. Bottom-line, Buddy-Boy: I neglected to honor the single most important gift in my lifetime. I took Nanny for granted when our two lives blended to one. We concentrated on meeting other people's expectations while we raised a family and built a career. I realize now, this time-honored excuse betrays trust and destroys the intimacy that keeps individuals connected as lovers and best friends."

My dog understands my truth. Buddy shows me the respect a mate displays for a partner. My Sweet-Boy does not denounce me this morning, and he does not console me. The Appalachian Trail is not the first wilderness passageway we've shared. There is nothing left to say. He simply lowers his head and returns to his breakfast. When Buddy-Boy finishes his food, my Labrador rests on the soil and gnaws a twig he holds between his front paws.

"How does a walk to Niday Shelter sound?" I ask Buddy, as I gather trash and put the stove, utensils, food, and water bottles in their assigned places in my backpack. "We can hike at an easy pace and arrive at Niday Shelter by mid-afternoon. The guidebook says the shelter is 10 miles and change from here. If we stick to the trail, we walk Cove Mountain's backside for two miles before we drop 800 feet in elevation to arrive at Trout Creek Footbridge. The pedestrian bridge is our first rest stop. Let's hope water flows underneath the walkway. We need to drink large quantities today to cut the dehydration symptoms we experienced yesterday. When our break ends, we climb 1,500 feet over four miles to the southern crest of Brush Mountain."

Buddy looks up when I describe the ascent to Brush Mountain's ridge.

"Don't fret, Big-Guy. The balance of today's hike looks reasonable. We walk the mountain ridgeline for a few miles before we eat lunch at the park bench marking the Audie Murphy Memorial Spur Trail. When we finish a light meal, we'll descend 1,500 feet to Craig's Creek and VA621. We'll hydrate and restore my water bottles at the stream, then wrap up the day with a 450-foot climb the last mile and a half to the shelter. Are you ready for day two, Sweet-Boy?"

"Poppy, I go where you lead. You sound eager to learn what the Appalachian Trail offers us. Let today's education begin."

My body delivered a marathon effort yesterday. The distinction between running a 26.2-mile race and hiking the Appalachian Trail is easy for me to explain. An endurance runner rests, then trains several weeks before the body is challenged to deliver another prolonged effort. When I get up from this picnic table, my dog and I must convince our minds to deliver 'marathon energy' today. I emphasize temperament, because our bodies will give up in this environment without a strong disposition.

Buddy and I are not in hiking shape. We will struggle with muscle soreness and mental fatigue in the early days. We can overcome our physical limitations by limiting miles each day for the first two weeks. If we stick to 10 miles a day, I believe we will survive without serious incident and be physically prepared to handle more distance in the tougher terrain.

Dehydration is an unexpected concern. Dehydration occurs when water loss overcomes water intake. I placed my dog and I in peril when I decided to ignore Central Virginia's heat and drought. We exited Adam's truck at the Catawba Trailhead; prepared for a walk-in-the-woods experience. Nature crushed me on this trail; behaving as a newcomer without a guide. If I want to stay in these mountains, I must show respect for the Appalachian Trail. Favorable regard for these mountains begins with proper hydration and nutrition habits.

I'm familiar with my physical limits after riding countless miles on my bicycle and running distance on the rolling streets and paths of Texas and Tennessee. When I ride my bike, I consume a bottle of fluid every hour and ingest quick-releasing carbohydrates every 45 minutes. When I run in the heat and humidity we encountered yesterday, I drink at least eight ounces of fluid an hour and keep up my carbohydrate routine. This will be my target intake, today.

Hydration maintenance is an obvious concern today. Central Virginia's drought is real, and the water is heavy. I know to drink a gallon of water blended with electrolytes each day to preserve fluid balance. Water weighs eight pounds per gallon. Buddy cannot carry the volume of liquid required to keep him hydrated. I've planned for Buddy to drink from the running streams we come across. I carry the smallest quantity I need to stay hydrated between water sources in this heat. If Buddy and I depend on fluid stored in my containers for two straight days, we are in trouble. The guide book says we can count on water sources today.

I've trained as an endurance athlete for a decade, avoiding acute injury by listening to my body. Muscles, tendons, and nerves tell me when I change technique, alter sleep regimen, vary hydration and nutrition protocol, wear deficient equipment, or push past fitness thresholds. Warnings always surprise me at inopportune moments. This morning fits the pattern. My right leg cramps from toe-tips to butt-cheek when I bend at the waist to pet Buddy.

Everyone cramps. I'm confident you recognize my discomfort and have a remedy. I hobble to the shelter and force myself to sit on the ground with my leg stretched, pressing my boot against a post supporting the shelter floor to release the pain and relax my muscles.

Buddy moves beside me to give aid. He places his head against mine and licks my cheek.

"Poppy, are you okay?"

I glance up to meet my Labrador's eyes.

"I'm visiting an old friend, Sweet-Boy. Give me a minute, okay?"

"Poppy, forget the minute. Let's take an unplanned rest day. We can relax, hydrate, and enjoy exploring the woods around Pickle Branch Shelter. Niday Shelter will wait for our arrival."

Common sense and good backcountry advice dissipates with the cramp in my leg.

"Buddy-Boy, remember, we work within an abbreviated hiking season. Don't worry—yesterday was an anomaly. We survived a formidable foe without training. I'll pay attention and stay hydrated. We'll be fine, today."

When I strap my pack to my back and my hiking poles are in hand, Buddy shakes his head, delivers a stern look, turns away from me, and walks up the trail on his own to start day two. I've frustrated my dog. He *should* be disappointed. I set aside my body's warning and didn't consider Buddy's physical condition when I made my choice. Fortunately, Buddy-Boy doesn't hold grudges. When we join up on the footpath, I try to earn his forgiveness.

"Hey Buddy, here is a compromise: after lunch, let's follow a blue blazed side trail to visit the Audie Murphy Monument."

Buddy looks at me with a puzzled expression.

"Who is Audie Murphy, Poppy?"

"Mr. Murphy was the most decorated U.S. Soldier during WWII. He was an authentic American hero. When the war was over, he used his celebrity status to become a movie actor. I wish you and I were friends when I was a young boy living in Russell, Kansas. I'd sneak you into the Saturday matinee at the *Dream Theater* to eat sunflower seeds and dill pickles while watching Audie Murphy star in war movies and cowboy films on the 'big screen'. Mr. Murphy died in a plane wreck on the mountain side we will walk near, today."

Buddy is spry this morning. His gate is strong, and his tail is wagging. He and I offset yesterday's wear and tear with a new confidence in our surroundings. The temperature is cool, and the hike is easy; descending at a moderate grade to Trout Creek.

This is my first experience using hiking poles on a backcountry walk. When I was agile, I accepted an occasional fall to avoid carrying ski poles to hike on dirt. Opinions change with age. I've learned hiking poles work as designed, once I adjust pole length to match topography and stride, and remember to remove the plastic cap secured to the point at the pole end.

This equipment provides essential benefits I missed on earlier hikes. My poles act as shoulder, arm, and hand extensions. They offer 'four legs' leverage maneuvering steep grade and rugged terrain. As important, the shafts reduce joint fatigue; redirecting shock that targets my ankles, knees, and hips each downhill step.

When I glance from the path between pole plants and footsteps this morning, my surroundings are striking. A mountain wall ascends skyward to my right and a mountain ravine falls to my left. Buddy and I stop when two deer break through the foliage below us. Buddy-Boy sits and enjoys the animals interact in their natural habitat. My dog does not bark, and he does not give chase. He is a respectful guest.

We arrive at the footbridge crossing Trout Creek before I remember to pull a water container from my backpack. I watch as Buddy explores the creek bank before he drinks from the active stream. When Buddy returns to my side, I cross the pedestrian bridge and walk away from this splendid water supply without touching my water bottles.

The real hiking day hits us straight in the face when we pass over a gravel road called 'VA620'. This is the Appalachian Trail. The climb to Brush Mountain's crest begins with a 1,100-foot net elevation gain the first mile of the trail. One day, I will daydream traveling mountain paths resembling Brush Mountain. Today is not that day. This isn't a walk. We are battling heat and terrain, plus yesterday's fatigue and dehydration symptoms.

The *Thru-Hikers' Companion* reports the next water source is seven miles away from Trout Creek. Adam suggested two miles per hour as a target pace while driving us to Catawba. I haven't produced two miles per hour since we stepped on the Appalachian Trail.

"Two water containers will not keep us hydrated," I admit to myself, leaning forward with my hands on my knees to catch my breath. "Here's the plan, Buddy-Boy: let's take our time to reduce calorie burn and body fluid consumption. We need to manage the water I carry to a half bottle when we reach the park bench leading to the Audie Murphy Monument. We will eat lunch and finish whatever's left in the container before we walk three miles to collect more water at Craig Creek. Two more miles on the trail and we arrive at Niday Shelter for the night. That is the strategy. Are you up for the challenge, Big-Guy?"

"Not to worry, Poppy. We survived Cove Mountain to Dragon's Tooth. Brush Mountain will be a walk-in-the-park. You lead the way."

Chapter Six
Brush Mountain Ridgeline

I've wondered how accomplished outdoorsmen stray into uncharted wilderness, never to be found. Disorientation caused by dehydration may be one reason.

I wander instead of hike with Buddy by my side. Our pace is less than a mile an hour. Dehydration symptoms dominate me. My ability to concentrate has diminished. I walk because my spirit tells my legs I must walk to survive. I do not sweat, and I do not remember the last time Buddy or I urinated.

The dirt path turns to a grass walkway at the approach to Brush Mountain summit, and the spur trail to Audie Murphy's monument. The corridor is as wide as a narrow, tree-lined fairway at an elite golf course. Grass is thick and tall; comparable to the fairway rough at the Masters Golf Tournament in Augusta, Georgia.

We must track trail signs to stay fixed to the Appalachian Trail. The minute I miss a white blaze, I know to turn around and retrace my steps. Not now. I quit tracking white paint when we stepped on the grass corridor.

"Buddy, this passageway is picturesque. I can't believe The Veterans of Foreign Wars forgot to replace the trail markers when they created this park setting as a lead to the Audie Murphy Monument."

The Veterans of Foreign Wars built the monument by his crash site around 1974. Thirty-plus years is plenty of time to brush new paint on trees. I'm so disoriented this minor detail never enters my thoughts.

My failure to hydrate myself yesterday has placed us in a dangerous predicament today. Buddy and I follow the golf course fairway without acknowledging a large sign commemorating Audie Murphy or the park bench at the spur trail leading to his monument. We descend Brush Mountain to the left as the Appalachian Trail descends the mountain to the right a mile behind us.

I believe we are safe. But we are actually in trouble. I'm lost walking the Brush Mountain Ridgeline.

The grass walkway ends at a paved parking surface serving a road covered with sharp, white stones. This encourages me. Based on the setting, this clearing is a high traffic trailhead. But it's not. The reality is: the paved surface is a parking lot supporting the Audie Murphy Monument, and the pathway is a service road that leads to Brush Mountain Road, not the Appalachian Trail.

If I am alert, I read my map, choose the best route to re-connect with the Appalachian Trail, and pray water runs through Craig Creek. I choose to investigate tree lines and side trails surrounding this parking lot for a trailhead or white paint designating the Appalachian Trail. No trailhead exists, and no paint is brushed on a tree or rock.

Buddy sits with me when I end my search and return to the place the greenbelt meets the gravel road. I'm convinced the Appalachian Trail intersects this road further down the mountain side.

"Buddy, I'm sorry I missed the trailhead leading to Craig Creek and Niday Shelter. We have two options: either we can follow this road downhill until it intersects the Appalachian Trail, or we can backtrack on the greenbelt to the trailhead I missed."

Simpsons Buddy-Boy leans forward and locks eyes with me. I'm confident Buddy is screaming, *"Poppy, we have one choice. We need to backtrack until we locate the Niday Shelter Trail Marker. Poppy, please study your map and make sure you are right before we take another step."*

More good counsel from a wise partner. I focus on Buddy instead of a map. I need to get my dog off this mountain, fast. Buddy's dry tongue hangs from his mouth. His chest moves with the rhythm of an overweight lineman whose completed his last wind sprint after a South Texas two-a-day football practice.

I'm confident this road will lead to civilization if it doesn't intersect with the Appalachian Trail. Choosing to walk this road may be the wrong choice, but it's not a fatal decision.

My dog is the better pathfinder, so I follow Buddy as he moves from side to side on the gravel road seeking smooth ground. I stay hopeful the Appalachian Trail intersection will appear after each bend in the road and each rise and fall in terrain.

The road surface is unfair to Buddy and aggravating for me. The rocks are sharp. Each step hurts, but Buddy doesn't complain. He finally balks when the roadside opens to an established maintenance yard containing surplus road material. I find soft ground covered with shade for Buddy to rest, then sit where he lays, offering him the best I can give: my affection, the small water supply that remains in my water bottle, and electrolyte powder he licks from my hand. I stroke Buddy's fur; massage his muscles and whisper soft words encouraging him to stay the fight with me.

Buddy's breathing calms, and he sleeps. I watch the sun drop closer to the horizon waiting for my dog to recover. Buddy eventually stands, and with my help, takes measured steps. When he walks with a gate resembling our new-normal pace, I return for his pack and follow his footsteps.

When we begin a hard descent around a hairpin turn, my dog forgets his physical condition, and runs straight for the woods. Buddy smells water before I see a shimmer from a surface interspersed with tree trunks. My disposition strengthens when Buddy enters the edge of the woods. I am devastated when he hits the surface and sinks to his chest in black goo.

I doubt I have the physical strength to wade in and pull Buddy out of this mess. Even if I can, I do not have the heart to stop him from drinking this oil-based slime. I am not joining Buddy in his play time, so I sit on the road and wait for my dog to quench his thirst and enjoy his black mud bath. When my Labrador finishes frolicking, he wages a minor war with sucking mud to get free.

My dog's hair is normally white, but now a happy animal with blackish-gray hair stands beside me wagging his tail.

"Good job, Gray-Dog. Way to kick the black slime's butt. You are such a good dog, Buddy-Boy. You saved me from wading in after you and contributing my socks and boots to the sucking mud's black abyss. Thank you, Warrior-Buddy!"

My sweet friend promptly returns my back-handed compliment. He shakes hard from nose to tail, showering me with a sticky wet viscous substance. This is Buddy's way of thanking me for missing the trail intersection and placing us in this precarious circumstance.

"Touché, Buddy."

After I place Buddy's pack on his back and adjust his straps, we continue slogging toward civilization. Our circumstance changes at sunset. My heart lightens when we walk around a bend in the rock road, miles from the paved parking lot. The road surface changes to compact material. Cattle are grazing in a green pasture fronting Brushy Mountain Road. The livestock feed behind a well-kept barbed wire fence. If you ask Buddy, he will tell you he guided us off Brush Mountain to civilization. I agree with him.

We carry out one survival tactic this afternoon. We stand on a paved road surface. This change in environment confirms my hope, but it's not a cause for celebration, yet. My dog is suffering, I am experiencing severe dehydration symptoms, and we stare at a field of cows in the middle of nowhere in Central Virginia.

With proper rest, I can navigate us back to the trail. I cannot recover without water for my dog and I. Without access to running water, my equipment and supplies are useless. I have been carrying air in my water bottles for hours, and the cell phone I depend on for emergencies does not carry a signal.

"Buddy-Boy, I'm running out of ideas. Walk for water is still my only solution for our problem." Buddy agrees with my assessment. He leaves my side and moves forward with a slow, heavy pace on the new road surface.

Before long, the smooth road bends at a hill crest and becomes a straight-away; revealing a road junction in the distance. Buddy picks up the pace and within 30 minutes, I see a human being walking on a property a quarter mile away.

My body tells me to run to the house and stick a water hose to my mouth without asking permission from the property owner. My pride will not allow me to admit defeat, yet. I am not ready to ask a stranger for help. I believe the abandoned house we walk by on the right-hand side of the road will have drinking water. Damn the "no trespassing" sign posted at the driveway.

As the sun drops low in the sky, I offer Buddy a solution, "Let's check out this abandoned property. Maybe this house has a hose bib we can use to fill our water bottles. If we find running water, we sleep here tonight. We will rest and figure out my mistake in the morning."

Buddy meets my eyes, then follows the driveway leading to the house. When I catch up, he is drinking from a pool of stagnant water in a deep tire track left in the driveway. I am not willing to get my water filtration gear out to pull this water for myself. I have hope for the house. We circle the abandoned residence twice without finding a source of fresh water.

"Buddy, who builds a house without an outdoor water faucet?" I ask, as we head back up the driveway to the main road.

We are in desperate straits. The sun sets below the horizon. I am homeless without access to water. I have no choice now. We walk to the property at the end of the road and I knock on a stranger's front door. I plan to beg for water for my dog and for me.

No answer. I knock again as barking erupts from the basement window beside the front door. I am ready to find a water hose in the front yard when a tall young man with a long pony tail walks around the side of his home.

"How can I help you, brother?"

Since Buddy and I communicate with thoughts, I rarely speak audibly. I want to tell this man I'm lost, and I will be happy to pay to use his water hose. I realize I am in dreadful shape when I speak garbled words to this friendly person.

The young man laughs, pulls me into a bear hug I'd expect to see a kinsman embrace a lost sibling with, and says, "Welcome home, brother. My name is Mark. You've experienced a long day. Follow me around the house where I can get you fresh water."

We gladly follow Mark to a nice side porch connected to his kitchen. Our host invites me to sit at an outdoor table as he enters his home. I take off my boots when he returns with an aluminum bowl full of water for Buddy. My socks are a bloody mess. Mark observes my predicament but holds any opinion to himself. I am too tired to care for my feet.

Mark is now in charge of us. He leaves and comes back with a glass of water he filled from his kitchen sink. He stands over me while I empty the container. This Good Samaritan retrieves the glass from me and returns with it full again. I drink this whole glass. Mark and I go through this "fill and drain" ritual for several minutes until I sense life return.

Mark refills Buddy's bowl and then joins me at the table. We discuss what occurred today and consider options to get back to the trail tonight. Mark doesn't belittle me in any way during our conversation. In fact, I am happy we followed the wrong passageway when he asks if I enjoy eating salad.

"Fresh greens are delicious," I answer.

"Good," he responds, as he goes into the kitchen to get a bowl, a knife, and a flashlight. Mark returns from the dark with a bowl full of greens, herbs, and other vegetables. He feeds Buddy dog food from his kitchen and then prepares me a fabulous garden-fresh salad with homemade dressing.

When I finish eating, I ask Mark for directions to the nearest shelter. Mark starts to answer my question, then changes his mind. He walks us to his tool shed and offers us a place to spend the night. I help arrange a sleeping space, and then Buddy and I shake Mark's hand.

"Jimmy Doug and Buddy, I'm setting soap and towels on the porch. You will find a water hose by the shed. Sleep well. I'll see you in the morning. Breakfast will be ready at 6:30. My daughter and I will drop you off at the Appalachian Trail on our way to school and work."

Mark's wife pulls in the driveway while I attend to my blistered feet. She is a school teacher. It has been a long day. She is kind and gracious to us as she heads into the house. Mark has many questions coming his way when she gets inside, but she makes us believe we are welcome when we are very vulnerable.

We are fortunate tonight. Day one did not break us. Day two came close. A stranger stopped his life to feed us and create a home for us when we could not take care of ourselves. Buddy tucks in next to me to share the warmth of my sleeping bag. We rest under a hard roof supported by walls. Two wood pallets elevate us from the ground. We are safe. Sleep arrives before the house lights extinguish.

Chapter Seven
Sinking Creek Mountain Ridgeline

Busy kitchen noise, tender words shared between a married couple, and light emitted from an active home briefly woke me up before dawn. I stir again when Mark's wife starts her car and backs out of the driveway before sunrise. She is beginning another day as a wife, a mother, a daughter, a teacher, and a gracious host to Buddy and me.

I rise from my sleeping pallet when her headlights disappear and put our packs back together. We sit at our familiar place on Mark's side porch when he steps through the kitchen door with a cup of black coffee.

"Good morning, Jimmy Doug and Buddy. Please come inside the house. Breakfast is ready. I want you both to meet my daughter, Emily."

The family residence is immaculate. Baked apples, scrambled eggs, bacon, hot biscuits, and orange juice cover the dining table. I never imagined I'd come upon a home while walking a wilderness path in solitude. Yet, here we are: two lost backpackers surrounded by a family's loving spirit. Emily is our hostess. She is a bright, happy little girl, who is delighted to have breakfast guests. Emily commands the morning, entertaining us from her highchair.

Day three's work begins as soon as Mark places his daughter in her car seat. I throw our packs and my hiking poles in the bed of Mark's truck, and Buddy leaps onto the pickup's open tailgate.

When Mark backs from the driveway onto the main road and speeds up, it's obvious that someone is late for work, school, or both. I snatch my ball cap from my head and grab the truck's side wall, praying Buddy and I survive this morning joy ride. I assume our trip will last a few minutes. When several minutes pass, I slide open the vehicle's back window and holler to Mark, "Next time I miss a trail intersection, I promise I'll turn around and retrace my steps."

He nods and laughs and continues to maneuver his truck through turns in the mountain roads. Mark didn't tell me, but we finished yesterday's hike over 180-degrees from our planned exit point. Brush Mountain blocks the path between his home and today's launching point. Mark loops around Brush Mountain's northern end and drives for a while before he abruptly stops by a clearing in the woods. Someone has abandoned a car in the small parking area. Mark jumps out of the pickup, helps me with the packs, and then points out the trail marker.

"Jimmy Doug, you are at the Craig Creek Road Trailhead. If I am not mistaken, you are 1.5 miles from the Niday Shelter. You know conditions are dry, so please take on water whenever you can."

Words cannot describe the gratitude and respect I hold for this stranger and his family. Mark took us into his life when we were desperate. Each member of his family treated us as invited guests they'd expected for months.

My emotions catch me unaware when Mark drives away and leaves us to find our own way again. Yesterday afternoon was brutal. I was frightened I was losing another life companion with nothing to offer but encouragement and presence. I suppressed my despair to concentrate on the job at hand, giving Buddy my best. It feels good to release these emotions this morning.

I'm not lonely and I am no longer hesitant. I am clean, energized, and ready for the next task.

"Buddy-Boy, time for work," I say, as I sit on a log by the trailhead to outline the day. I laugh when Buddy sits by my side and leans forward with me to study the map I unfold and lay on the ground. He follows my finger trace where I made my navigating mistake yesterday, where we are now, and the path we will follow today to Sarver Hollow Shelter.

Mark has dropped us off on 'VA621' at Lee Hollow. Craig's Creek is behind us, a quarter mile to the north. We need to walk a mile to reach Niday Shelter. When we finish studying the map, I put it away and open the *Thru-Hikers' Companion*. My dog stretches out on the ground and licks his front paws as I absorb information I receive from this reference book.

"Buddy-Boy, the guidebook reports water at Niday Shelter and at a stream we cross a mile from Niday Shelter. That will be it for our water resources until we reach Sarver Hollow Shelter. Sarver Hollow is 4.5 miles from the last stream."

Buddy doesn't react to information reported in the book. He heard the water story yesterday. I know his thoughts, *"Poppy, I'm trusting feet on the ground. I'm drinking water when I see water."*

"You are right, Buddy. I'll follow your lead today. Just so you understand, Sweet-Boy, I appreciate you jumping from Mark's truck to join up with me. The first two days have been humdingers. I'd understand if you preferred to stay with Mark's family."

"Poppy, you still don't understand. I volunteered long ago to love you and protect you wherever you go. If you want to hike the Appalachian Trail, I will walk with you."

I hug my dog long and hard before I inspect his body for hotspots and each foot pad for abrasions. He is in good shape considering the miles he walked on sharp rock. I'm not so lucky. Last night, I discovered blisters on both heels and the balls of both my feet plus on the tips of three toes on my right foot. I am troubled when I check my feet now.

"Buddy, these blisters are pathetic. Why are my heavy hiking boots failing me on this trip? I didn't suffer a single blister the last three backpacking ventures I wore these boots and socks."

Buddy stares toward me with compassion, then he licks my arm to let me know he senses my pain. I describe the morning challenge while I lift my heavy pack onto my shoulders and bend at the waist to pull the straps.

"No warm-up this morning, Buddy-Boy. We start with a 450-foot climb to Niday Shelter. Then, we ascend another 1,400-foot rise over 2.5 miles to reach the north-end of Sinking Creek Mountain Ridgeline."

These are sobering words for an aging athlete to take in after two days of physical pounding. Buddy is a hunting dog. He's bred to work at a high level in difficult circumstances. He checks with me to make sure I have my hiking poles in hand before we start up the trail.

"Poppy, how can you expect a lesser challenge? This is the Appalachian Trail. We stand in a valley surrounded by mountainsides that measure us as insignificant. Let's go."

"Lead the way, Buddy. Stop me when we get to Sarver Hollow Shelter," I laugh, accepting my track record, then drop my head and follow my dog's familiar gait.

Adam told me to expect "trail angels" on the Appalachian Trail. Trail angels are individuals who arrive in a hiker's life at unsuspected times to deliver welcome acts of kindness with nothing required in return. Mark and his family are the first trail angels I have come upon in the Jefferson National Forest.

Adam didn't tell me spirits or ghosts exist on these mountain paths. As we walk, I recall several entries posted on the internet by Appalachian Trail Hikers recording personal encounters with a ghost at Sarver Hollow Shelter.

"Do apparitions interest you, Buddy?" I ask, as we struggle up the hill to Niday Shelter. "I have never seen a ghost. Have you?"

Buddy turns his head without breaking stride to glance my way but doesn't answer my question.

We are tired and thirsty when we reach Niday Shelter. I take off our packs and Buddy moves to the water source below the shelter. I relax on the picnic table for a few minutes, reading the shelter's trail journal and sipping my water. A female thru-hiker passed through this location several days before our arrival. Complaints saturate her journal entry. She describes water shortages on the trail and hiking alone for several days. This thru-hiker doesn't write the word, but it's obvious she is lonely. Two male southbound thru-hikers follow her entry with their own stories. Based on their writings, the female hiker will have companions before long. As I close the notebook and slide it back in the waterproof sleeve, my guess is they are together now, hiking as a team.

When I return the trail journal to its safe place in the shelter, I follow the blue blaze trail Buddy used to find water. I finish drinking my first bottle at the creek and then re-fill it with my filtration equipment. Neither one of us is in a hurry this morning. We relax and enjoy the critters playing on their home turf. When we are ready to face the big climb to Sinking Creek Mountain's ridgeline, we walk back to the shelter, put on our packs, and leave Niday Shelter.

Breaks in the tree canopy show heavy clouds suspended across the blue sky.

"Hey Buddy, check out the thunderclouds filling the skyline. If we are lucky, rain will fall today and restock the dry creek beds with drinking water."

My dog looks up, sniffs the air, then swings around me and sets a strong pace. Rain is coming.

Backcountry walks are fun. I come and go, carrying life necessities on my back as I track proven trails to safe dwellings built by someone else. It's difficult to imagine the challenge fearless men married to stronger women overcame to carve out a living and make a home for their families in this forest.

"Buddy, can you envision living here year-round, maintaining a homestead, and raising a family? The Sarver family remained 70 years on the land we sleep on tonight. Volunteers built Sarver Hollow Shelter on their homestead. My reading says Henry Sarver raised his family in a two-story cabin he built before the Civil War. The Sarver's earned a living on their land until the Great Depression ended. When the economy recovered, they turned their back on a furnished cabin, never to return.

"You've watched me and Reece move furniture from a second story house to a moving van. Can you imagine trying to transport two stories of furniture by hand from this mountain to the valley? I agree with Old Henry. Pack out what you can on your back and build new when you reach the new homestead.

"They say the cabin is in ruins now, but the fireplace chimney remains intact. The family cemetery still exists. I say we visit the old homestead after we get settled into the shelter this afternoon."

Buddy doesn't cast a vote. He suffers in silence this morning. He hasn't acknowledged one question. I'm not sure he is even listening. The hard work we endured the first two days has taken a toll, and now we're forced to swallow the bitter cocktail I've mixed: backpack weight, physical exhaustion, and extreme incline. My legs burn from the effort required to push myself uphill. Strap adjustments are futile. Nothing stops the searing pain in my shoulders. How we choose matters. I regret the decision to pack for comfort instead of necessity.

As I struggle to talk and climb, I work to finish telling Buddy the Sarver Hollow story.

"The legend is: a Sarver family member has chosen the old homestead as their heaven. Buddy-Boy, I must tell you, it's been hard for me to discount the legend after I read the different encounters hikers have shared with the ghost at Sarver Hollow. Who knows, maybe we'll meet a Sarver tonight."

I end my one-sided chat with those words. I need to concentrate on the path ahead. The trail demands my full strength to pull against the ground with hiking poles, and push with burning calves, thighs, and butt muscles to get up this grade. Sweat soaks my clothes and boots when we finish climbing 720 feet in less than a mile.

I am tired and complaining to myself when the passageway completes a sweeping turn across the mountainside. The footpath teases me with a false-flat imitating the Sinking Creek Mountain Ridgeline. I'm grateful for this small reprieve from all the suffering I've endured. My body relaxes as my mind prepares to walk this ridgeline to Sarver Hollow Shelter. The mountain unveils its cruel joke when the trail kicks skyward and forces us to ascend another 700 feet to reach the actual ridgeline.

As we begin this ascent, I turn back and smile at Buddy.

"Stay focused on the prize, Pal. Our second water stop is close. The quicker we climb this incline, the sooner we can rest, hydrate, and enjoy a snack."

I make a promise I can't keep. My resilience falters when we complete the climb and cross the dry creek bed serving as today's second water source. We now hike a third day on this drought-ridden trail without hydrating. I don't panic, but I am flustered. I find a rock next to a large tree on the edge of the trail and plant my butt on the stone with a thud. When my backpack is off, I rest my equipment against the rock, slide to the ground, lean my body against the tree, and pout.

Buddy finds a shady spot in the dirt further up the trail. He rests on his forelegs and waits. He is confident. I appreciate the trail advice I believe he offers to improve my sorry outlook.

"Change your socks, Poppy. You need a distraction."

I remove my wet boots and sweat-drenched socks. The last time I saw blisters comparable to mine I helped friends carry another hiker's backpack out of the Alaskan wilderness.

Adam educated me on backcountry medicine before I left Roanoke. I can hear him encouraging me now, "Jimmy Doug, superglue is the perfect solution for blisters and cuts. Please make sure you carry a large container of the liquid adhesive in your first aid kit."

My medical supplies lie at the bottom of my pack. As I pull out food and equipment, I recognize the extra weight I haul up these mountainsides: a one-degree sleeping bag I purchased for Alaska I carry in this heat, a new tent I tote when I plan to sleep in shelters, an air mattress I transport that doesn't hold air, and extra food and clothes I know I won't need before I resupply.

I clean my wounds when I secure my medical supplies. This time, I apply a generous quantity of superglue over each blister. I have a plan when I pull dry socks over new band aids attached to strong liquid adhesive. I will play Santa Claus in September and leave "Ho-Ho-Ho, Merry Christmas" gifts on the side of the Appalachian Trail for someone stronger than me to carry today.

Buddy stares in disbelief as I stack the needless weight I carry in my backpack beside the tree trunk. He stands to stop me when he sees me walk away with my pack on my back.

"Poppy, wake up. You must be sleep walking. You've stacked my food and your equipment beside the dirt path."

I know this behavior is crazy. In two weeks, I will return to the Outfitter in Salem, Virginia, with a broken big toe and dead toe nails super glued to three toes. The outfitter will accept the $569 I gladly spend to replace my sleeping bag, air mattress, and tent with ultra-light equipment. My concerns are equipment weight and making it through this day on these feet, not dollars.

"What are you staring at, Big-Boy? Don't worry, you have plenty of food. Do you want to trade packs since I've lightened my load?" I tease, smiling at my companion.

Buddy waits for me to pass and then he falls in behind me without making another sound.

People ask me, "How are you?" without waiting to listen for an honest response. Folks are busy. They have problems. Time is a gift they do not waste on someone else's trouble. I know this. That's why I respond, "I'm okay" when someone takes the time to share a pleasant greeting.

What does "I'm okay" mean walking backcountry trails? After three days, "I'm okay" means I am moving to water; I am thirsty and exhausted. Buddy and I are okay when we reach Sinking Creek Mountain Ridgeline.

The footpath follows a thick wall of vegetation that guides us along the mountain edge. Breaks in foliage occur from time to time to present dramatic rock formations extending beyond the mountain side. Buddy walks right by me and sits when we reach one of these outcroppings. I often wonder what he considers staring across these open spaces. These distractions make our physical discomfort inconsequential compared to the grandeur present in our circumstances.

I appreciate the lessons the Appalachian Trail teaches. This national treasure tests my skill and perseverance the same as a major league batter confronts a major league pitcher. Pitchers keep hitters "off-balance" mixing in sliders, change-ups, and an occasional curveball with their fastballs. The Appalachian Trail keeps thru-hikers off-balance mixing in diverse grade with assorted terrain and changing weather. The terrain we walk this afternoon pitches a big change from dirt to large slabs of solid rock.

This switch in landscape is a welcome relief. Smooth rock, set against the open sky means we are free from the emotional weight I endure under the tree canopy. Freedom's price? We negotiate lengthy stretches of slick stone sitting on grade tilted left toward the ravine. Rock staircases separate the pitched slab sections.

Buddy sits by my side, facing the first section with me. I'm nervous. Buddy takes the point when we walk on dirt footpaths. I wish he'd lead now, but he won't. I try to mask my apprehension with humor.

"Buddy, where's the safety barrier? It's a long fall to the ravine floor if I slip and slide on this slick stone."

My dog smiles and drags a paw across the rock.

"Poppy, extend your hiking pole for added leverage and take small steps. Be patient and you will be fine."

I purchased my boots in Arizona. I felt safe wearing a daypack and climbing across red rock in Sedona, Arizona. Several hikes included challenges similar to this grade and surface. Since my boots are old, I fall hard and slide fast, varying distances several times throughout the afternoon.

Buddy-Boy is always respectful. He waits until I finish crossing a rock section before he traverses the surface on his own. It is a pleasure to see Buddy work this terrain. He makes a task look easy using his intelligence, strength, and agility. I envy his ability to rely on a low center of gravity and four feet to navigate the slick rock.

When I buy a new pair of boots, we will blow right through comparable sections on the Appalachian Trail. When isn't now, and I am concerned for my safety. Fatigue, thirst, and challenging rock formations are combining to create another dangerous environment for us.

On a whim, I pull out my phone and push the on button. To my surprise, I have a signal, so I call my best friend in Texas. Reece answers her phone and we have an encouraging conversation. She is interested in our progress and concerned for our safety. I stress the problem we face finding water on the trail. I believe Reece is kidding when she tells me with great confidence:

"Jimmy Doug, I will take care of that problem for you."

Reece does not tell me on the phone, but she is monitoring the weather in our vicinity. When Buddy and I reach the next open plateau, we watch a long line of thunderstorms move our way. The rain is welcome. The lightning is troubling. I spend the next hour studying the thunderstorm approach through breaks in vegetation fencing the ridgeline, hopeful we will find cover to protect ourselves from the storms punishing elements. When we reach the next open space on the trail, I drop to a knee and ask Buddy to come sit facing me.

"Buddy-Boy, we can't avoid lightning strikes and high winds on this ridgeline. It's your choice, Sweet-Boy; either we can walk this difficult terrain in hard rain or we can stop and have fun. Want to build a rain-catcher to gather water? I can cover our equipment and my clothes to keep them dry, then we can lay on a rock and enjoy a good soaking while my poncho traps drinking water."

Buddy's eyes sparkle. My Labrador wants to catch water to drink from the sky. I agree. When rain clouds block sunlight, creating shadows on the valley floor, we execute our plan. We are lucky this afternoon. Big, dark clouds deliver rain without lightning or high winds. Our plan works, and we have a great time. I encourage everyone to remove their clothes and experience rain beat against their bare skin, at least once in their life.

Buddy is drinking from the water pocket resting in my poncho while I reach for the towel I set aside to dry off our bodies. I smile when I see his eyes are happy. Water drips from my dog's chin as he lifts his head to glance my way,

"Poppy, come drink this water with me. We built this together."

"You enjoy yourself, Sweet-Boy. You've earned this treat. I will find water for myself later," I tell Buddy, as he takes pleasure drinking the fresh rainwater.

The rain dissipates in tandem with the increase in temperature and humidity. The sun shows no mercy reflecting off white slabs of stone. I don't understand why the sun doesn't evaporate a film of moisture from the trail's stone surface. My earlier efforts negotiating the slabs were comical. My skill level is now ridiculous. Unfortunately, the pain attached to each slip and slide makes it difficult to laugh at myself. I know I should stay on hands and knees to move across the tilted slabs, but I can't make myself crawl for this trail.

Buddy copes with his own challenges. He is laboring in the heat and humidity. We are fortunate the rain shower deposited gifts of water for my dog to drink in small pockets of rock surface and in bowls created by fallen leaves. The hunt for water in obscure receptacles provides enough liquid to keep Buddy moving. The search for this hidden treasure helps us view our environment at a micro level. This simple change in perspective creates a fun distraction we share until we reach the tree canopy and say goodbye to the white stone slabs and the rough rock stairs.

Chapter Eight
Sarver Hollow Apple Orchard

We walk with a comfortable gait at a faster pace on the forest floor's flat surface. Nature's turned down the dimmer switch. The further we walk under the tree canopy, the gloomier our surroundings become. Life experience says heavy thunderclouds are overhead.

"Buddy, a new line of thunderstorms has arrived. Next time I call Reece and complain we are short on water, I'll make sure we have a hard roof over our heads."

No response.

I notice a life pattern present itself in wilderness solitude. Buddy treats me the same as Reece and my children. He ignores me when I mumble idle words, flowing from an active mind to break the silence.

As I set this thought free, Buddy releases a muffled bark and slips by me on the trail. This behavior must be his new response to my distracting chatter. I'm not prepared to stop when he sits to block the trail. I slam my hiking poles into the ground to break my fall. When I regain my balance, I see a tall young man dressed in unique clothes standing beside the trail's edge. The gentleman offers a friendly smile as he waits for us to pass by him on the walking path. I introduce myself as Buddy extends his own friendly greeting to the stranger.

"Is there a handy water source nearby?" I ask the stranger, forgetting my manners. I should have waited for the man to introduce himself before I asked my question. *"To hell with manners,"* I chuckle under my breath. *"I'm thirsty."*

"Hello Jimmy Doug and Buddy. I'm Phillip," the stranger responds, joining my laughter. "I've been at Sarver Hollow picking apples. You will find a ground well behind Sarver Hollow

Shelter. Water seeps from the ground, but I believe you can drink the stagnant fluid once you boil it or treat it with iodine tablets."

After Phillip answers my question, he explains why he's on this path today.

"The last time I crossed this section of trail, the white slabs gave me fits. It's time to test myself again, before I return to the shelter."

I smile without speaking. Perhaps the white slabs are slick and dangerous, and I am not the klutz I believe I am today.

"Good luck, Phillip. Nice meeting you," I say, as I turn back to the trail and head Buddy south toward the shelter.

"Jimmy Doug, be careful walking in this rain," Phillip responds before he heads north toward the open terrain. "Buddy, I will see you soon. Keep an eye on Jimmy Doug till I get back. This storm will deliver hard rain with strong winds and lightning on this ridgeline."

As Phillip turns to leave, I see he carries an empty backpack. I can't place the clothes he wears. The style and cloth are from a different era, worn in a different climate. My gut sends a tingle through my spine. My spirit is alert.

"It doesn't matter what the stranger wears or carries in his pack," I conclude. *"Phillip is friendly enough, and he walked away from us."* Facts I recite to calm my inquisitive mind.

"Maybe it doesn't matter," I add. *"But why is he here, walking a ridgeline with this thunderstorm approaching? Why is he headed out into the open now, to walk across those rocks in the rain, wind, and lightning?"* I speculate.

"Buddy, I don't remember a story describing an apple orchard at Sarver Hollow. Phillip isn't carrying apples in his pack. It's possible he left fresh fruit at the shelter," I say aloud, as the first burst of thunder rolls overhead.

Thirty to forty minutes pass and rain falls hard enough to penetrate the tree canopy with force. Buddy and I stop, and I wave when we hear Phillip's voice cut through the rainfall. I assume Phillip has cut short his rendezvous with the slick white rock slabs. Phillip approaches us and then stops at a safe distance from me as Buddy sits at attention by my side.

My dog notices a change in Phillip's countenance. Buddy approaches and delivers a friendly greeting to a good person who does not threaten his family or his home. Buddy knows Phillip, and he does not move to greet the man.

"How was your reunion on the rocks, Phillip?"

"The rock slabs were easy today, Jimmy Doug. I don't understand why I had trouble the last time I crossed them."

"Did you walk the path to the north end?"

"I did. When the sky turned dark, I ran the ridgeline to beat the rain. I didn't fall one time."

"Good for you, Phillip," I say, calling bullshit under my breath.

I am cautious in wilderness settings whether I stand in a boardroom or the backcountry. A person earns my confidence before I allow them into my personal space. I trust Buddy to judge the spirit that hides behind a person's friendly face. My dog stays put by my side. If Phillip is a liar, he's a good liar. This stranger gives me the impression he is telling the truth. He is in a good mood, adopting a relaxed stance with his legs shoulder-width apart. He never pulls his eyes from mine when he speaks.

Phillip wears a mountaineer hat, a wool coat with open buttons, corduroy pants, a handmade leather belt with a unique buckle, and handmade deerskin moccasins. What interests me most is how this friendly man stands in the rain, on an isolated mountain ridgeline, with a handmade "Bowie Knife" size weapon tucked between his belt and his pants. *Why does this stranger linger? I wish he'd pass us and go on with his day.*

Phillip's story was a challenge to accept when we met him. What concerns me the most is how his hand remains resting on the hilt of the knife.

"Buddy, can we trust this man?" My dog does not move from my side to block our path and he does not move forward to greet the stranger he welcomed earlier.

"Thanks, Pal."

I stand in the rain wearing a heavy pack, worn out from three days full of hard effort. Now, I face a young man whose hand rests on a large knife. A stranger with a formidable weapon my dog will not approach.

I try to give Buddy multiple options when we face new challenges. Since I will not turn my back on this stranger to continue our hike, my options are these: reach for Buddy's pack and pull out the big knife Adam insisted I carry or ignore the knife Phillip carries and look this young man straight in the eyes without fear. I can prepare to fight Phillip and lose my life, or I can stand in the rain with Phillip until he's ready to move.

I decide I'll offer a friendly smile and continue to display a genuine interest in the stranger's story. When my countenance changes, Buddy moves forward and welcomes Phillip into our circle. Buddy makes a good choice.

The thunderstorm is unyielding. The Appalachian Trail changes from footpath to mountain gutter filled with fast-moving water. Deep mud forms on each side of the passageway, forcing our little group to trek the submerged walkway. I lead, Buddy follows, and Phillip brings up the rear.

The storm's noise level is alarming. I acknowledge danger when lightning strikes close by on both sides of the trail. I should be afraid for my life, but fear does not penetrate my consciousness. Phillip's presence has a calming effect. He keeps us distracted, sharing his extensive knowledge of geology in this region.

Phillip startles me when he walks by my side and shouts:

"Jimmy Doug, I am worried Buddy is sick. He needs medical care. It's important you get him off the trail tomorrow. With your permission, may I carry Buddy's pack for him to the shelter?"

Phillip poses this gracious act of kindness in this horrific storm with humility and politeness. He exhibits a level of respect I will soon learn is the normal way hikers speak on the Appalachian Trail.

"Thank you, Phillip. Let me help you with his pack."

Phillip opens his empty backpack while I remove the water-soaked equipment Buddy carries with pride and without complaint. I witness relief in my dog's eyes as I lift the pack's weight off his shoulders and hips. Phillip slides Buddy's equipment into his backpack as I express deep gratitude to the second helping stranger we have encountered on this short journey.

The rain is unrelenting. The tree canopy cannot hold back the downpour. Visibility is poor as the wilderness' afternoon light turns the shade of late dusk. I'm concentrating on foot placement as water streams from my ball cap's bill when I hear Phillip shout out to get my attention.

"Jimmy Doug, you missed the turnoff to Sarver Hollow."

I'm surprised, but not embarrassed that I walked right by the wooden sign in this weather. I retrace my steps and watch Phillip and Buddy through a sheet of rain descend the side trail leading to Sarver Hollow Shelter.

The path is narrow. The grade is steep. And footing is treacherous. Phillip negotiates this topography same as a sunny day. Buddy is confident following his new friend.

Given the extreme conditions, I should measure every downhill foot placement. But I don't. My imagination runs wild as soon as Phillip grabs an object from the ground resembling a rifle. I stay fixated on the weapon I believe Phillip is carrying. When we reach the shelter, torrential rain turns to a light mist, and Phillip places a long piece of bark on the picnic table.

"I hope you don't mind, Jimmy Doug. Bark works as a makeshift shovel. You can use this tool to improve flow in the water box behind the shelter."

"Good idea," is my best response. Caution is a virtue when you hike alone. I judged Phillip based on fear. Trust earned is trust valued. I trust this stranger.

"Jimmy Doug, let me show you the water box and the homestead at the back of the property."

I follow Phillip and Buddy along a fading path with my water bottles, my cook pot, and my water filtration gear. My hiking companions turn into a small grove of trees where Buddy disappears into the ground. When I arrive, Buddy-Boy stands at the bottom of a water box framed on three sides by brown stone walls. Brown stone stairs secure the entry side. I pause beside Phillip and admire Buddy drinking quiet water seeping into the rock box from under the back wall.

"Why is it animals can drink water I have to boil or treat before I drink from the same source?"

Phillip glances my way and shrugs his shoulders. Buddy doesn't lift his head to answer my question.

When Buddy quenches his thirst, Phillip leads us to the back of the property. He tells the Sarver Family story as he points out the cemetery, the cabin remains, and a stand of trees that are apple free today.

When Phillip concludes the tour, light rain falls again and the dark approaches fast. I'm grateful our hiking day has concluded. Thick clouds and heavy rainfall will restrict night vision, making treacherous descents dangerous. Phillip places his hand on my shoulder as I turn toward the shelter.

"Jimmy Doug, it's time for me to leave. Thank you for sharing the afternoon with me."

Phillip's statement surprises me, but I stay quiet. I am learning Appalachian Trail etiquette: Phillip speaks for himself and decides for himself. He lives with his choice; I don't.

Buddy's aware his friend is leaving Sarver Hollow. He moves to Phillip's side to say, "thank you" and "goodbye" in his way. Phillip reminds me to get Buddy off the trail tomorrow. We shake hands and he wishes us both good travels.

When we finish exchanging goodbyes, Buddy and I watch Phillip walk into the stand of apple trees. He vanishes in the landscape before our eyes. Phillip's departure reminds me of the ballplayers who disappeared into the stand of corn in Kevin Costner's movie: *Field of Dreams*. Angel or trail angel, I do not know the answer. I believe what I saw at the Sarver Hollow apple orchard.

"Buddy, did you see what I saw?"

Buddy responds with a "yes", dragging his paw against my leg.

I suspect Phillip dropped from sight at an abrupt change in elevation I can't distinguish from this distance. A vehicle surely waits for Phillip on a gravel road at the bottom of this mountainside.

My question is this: how does a man manage the 1,000-foot rain-drenched drop he will navigate in pitch-black to reach the valley floor? Phillip does not carry night vision equipment. If the Sawyer's carved a proven trail into the mountainside, Phillip will still need unique climbing skill to escape this peril unscathed.

How else can I explain Phillip's presence and departure?

Buddy stands motionless, staring after Phillip for a time I do not measure. I wonder what Buddy can distinguish. I'll never know, and the answer doesn't matter. This stranger was our trail angel this afternoon. I will always remember with gratitude the gifts of confidence, knowledge, and kindness he shared with us out of personal sacrifice with nothing expected in return.

I stay quiet beside Buddy, absorbing the spirit covering the family homestead. A couple raised children and prospered here. I honor the Sarver Family, this evening.

"Thank you, Phillip. I hope we see you, again," I say to myself, turning for the shelter to begin my evening chores.

Chapter Nine
Sarver Hollow Shelter

My headlamp works as designed in the secure confines of this three-sided shelter built to accommodate around six hikers. Buddy makes himself comfortable on the wood planked floor. I grab a towel and wipe his white coat to soothe his spirit and relax his muscles. When my Labrador closes his eyes to rest, I prepare his evening meal then secure the collapsible container he carries in his pack to store large quantities of water. Buddy doesn't budge when I call his name and place his food bowl by the picnic table. He stays put when I take the digging tool Phillip provided and the water bag back to the water box. He doesn't get up to greet me when I return and hang our water supply on a hook nailed to a wall.

I remove his food bowl from the ground beside the picnic table and place it under his nose. Buddy ignores his food. He doesn't respond to my touch when I stroke his hair and massage his shoulders, back strap, and hips. My dog is exhausted. He gave his best to help me walk 30 miles to Sarver Hollow Shelter.

Since my sleeping bag is in someone else's pack, I spread out my sleeping bag liner on top of the poncho I place on the wooden floor. I double over my ground cover and lay it over the sleeping bag liner to create my bed for the night.

Buddy sleeps while I change into dry clothes, then I hang the wet clothes and equipment on hooks attached to the board holding up the shelter's open face wall. I am boiling water on my portable stove when I hear the words:

"Hello, in the shelter," pierce through the rain and darkness.

Buddy lifts his head and cocks his ears to alert me a new voice has entered our living space. When he has my attention, he moves to my sleeping pad and secures a comfortable spot to watch over me. He does not rise to greet our visitors. This is odd behavior for my friendly and protective dog. I turn off the stove, set the boiling water to the side, and step around the shelter to add light from my headlamp to the footpath.

"Welcome home," I shout into the downpour from underneath the roof's eve.

Rain streams off Daniel and Jordan when they step on the shelter porch, one at a time; five minutes apart. These men are young, energized, southbound thru-hikers. Daniel's trail name is Bernie. He began his personal journey in New Jersey. Jordan's trail name is Sidestep. He began his journey in Pennsylvania.

Jordan greets Buddy while he removes his backpack.

"Hello Big-Dog. Want a treat?" he asks, reaching into his pack's side pocket for a piece of jerky.

Buddy raises his head and attempts to wag his tail, but he does not rise to greet this friendly stranger. I've never seen my dog ignore a treat.

"Labradors are friendly animals," Jordan tells me. "What's wrong with your dog?"

"Nothing is wrong with Buddy, Jordan. He's had a tough day. He's a friendly, well-mannered soul. I'm confident Buddy will challenge you for your breakfast in the morning," I say with a smile on my face.

Daniel brings positive energy to the building when he arrives. He pulls off his backpack, places his equipment on the shelter floor, shakes off the wetness beside the picnic table, and shares a cheerful greeting. When he sees my Labrador, he exclaims, "Dog!" then hops onto the shelter floor and walks straight to Buddy.

"How are you, Buddy-Boy? Did you have a rough day?" he asks, as he gently rubs my dog's ears and strokes his face.

Buddy lifts his head and licks Daniel's arm before he settles back into my sleeping pad.

"What's wrong with Buddy, Jimmy Doug?"

"I'm not sure, Daniel. We are newcomers to the AT. We've walked from Catawba to this shelter the last three days. Buddy and I are tired and sore. I'm uncomfortable because my fitness level is poor. I eat, but Buddy, who is a better-conditioned athlete than me, won't touch his food. We haven't met our hydration requirements, but Buddy's consumed a larger quantity of fluid per pound of body weight than me. I'm sure I'm suffering minor dehydration symptoms, but they haven't affected my appetite. Buddy's dehydrated, but I believe he's also presenting flu symptoms.

"The distinction between me and Buddy is the fluid he engulfed yesterday and this evening: oil-based slime, putrid water in a tire track, and standing water in the ground well behind this shelter. I'd have a stomach ache drinking like Buddy. I hope he hasn't ingested poison."

"Sweet-Dog," Daniel says, giving his complete attention to Buddy-Boy. "Rest well this evening, Big Dog. Jordan and I will watch over Dad for you. The creeks and streams will fill tonight. Find your strength and let your body heal. Tomorrow will deliver new adventures to enjoy."

Buddy lifts himself from the floor when Daniel finishes sharing these encouraging words. He hugs Daniel and then slowly proceeds to his food bowl. After he eats a few bites, he hops back onto the shelter floor and returns to my sleeping pallet.

Unplanned circumstances have forced seasoned thru-hikers to share a cabin in the woods with a newcomer nursing a sick dog. As Buddy listens from his position on the shelter floor, these young men share today's highlights. Both departed from Pickle Branch Shelter early this morning. They describe the Audie Murphy Monument for me and explain details I missed leading to the Niday Shelter trailhead. These men are confident, conditioned athletes who crossed Sinking Creek Mountain's ridgeline at dusk in a rainstorm and walked in one day what has taken me two days to travel.

Both men are efficient at creating their shelter space, handling wet equipment and clothes, cooking their evening meal, finding time to relax, and preparing for bed. They are grateful but cautious when I offer them access to the water hanging from my bag on its hook. These two males do not know me. Jordan is careful with the water. He makes sure he understands the source before he accepts the gift. He boils the water before filling his hydration resources. Daniel uses his filtration equipment to draw water from the bag. I chuckle to myself when Daniel lays out his sleeping bag. September Santa Claus visited this young man today.

Buddy lies next to me under our ground cover. He can't stop shivering. I massage his body until his muscles stop shaking. Buddy moves closer when I rest my arm across his torso.

"I will get you to an animal doctor after breakfast," I whisper to my friend.

I fall asleep holding my dog.

If a ghost is moving around Sarver Hollow Shelter tonight, we are too tired to wake up and greet him. My guess, "The ghost of Sarver Hollow" went home tonight, soaked and muddy, to eat dinner with his girlfriend at an apartment by the Virginia Tech Campus. I'm just guessing.

When I open my eyes to greet day four, Daniel and Jordan are busy completing their morning chores. The energy they generate reminds me of years I enjoyed helping my children prepare for school. There's no reason to interfere with these men's morning routine, so I sit against the back wall and watch them while I enjoy a daydream connected to my son and daughter, sharing this morning with their children.

Maybe that's the answer, I half-joke to myself. *My heart is heavy because I'm starving for my grandchildren's attention.*

"Buddy-Boy, let's head home after your veterinary appointment. Then we will enjoy life with my grandchildren."

When I glance toward Buddy, his sweet eyes stare through me.

"No, Poppy. We will visit the animal doctor today and then come back to the trail. We are hiking the Appalachian Trail for us and the family. When we finish, we go home. And Poppy, finish means more than miles. You are a good man. I believe in you. Believe in yourself. Let's use this time wisely."

Buddy knows my heart. I lean in his direction and whisper, "You're right, Buddy."

Buddy rests his torso against my leg and relaxes his muscles. When he's settled, I rub his shoulders and softly communicate today's plan.

"Buddy, time and water aren't issues, today. Let's plan for a short hike."

I laugh when Buddy raises his head with eyes wide open.

"Buddy, I'm kidding. When the guys leave, we'll check the map and guide book to find the quickest way to get you to a veterinarian."

When I finish whispering to him, he fills his massive lungs with air, extends his nose to my cheek and exhales his stale breath straight into my face.

"My friend: Buddy-Boy," I laugh to myself, rubbing my eyes and wiping dog breath off my skin. I understand my life companion. Satisfied with his prank, Buddy will lay by my side and wait for me to begin our day.

It's interesting to see Daniel and Jordan skirt around the cabin to finish their tasks. They work in tandem in different space, completing separate tasks. One moment, the shelter is chaotic. The next instant, the two men are standing together with packs on their backs and hiking poles in hands. Daniel wears running shorts and a wicking shirt. Jordan wears a do-rag over his shaved head and elastic braces on his knees and ankles. Daniel carries a Ukulele strapped to his pack.

Both men talk nonstop while they eat breakfast and hydrate, refill their hydration resources, pack their bags, treat minor medical issues, visit the outhouse, and then put on wet clothes and boots. I listen while Jordan cusses the strap that rips from his backpack. This is the second pack he has carried on this journey and the second strap he's pulled from this pack. Anyone within shouting distance of the shelter hears their lively discussion on the merits of taking a side trip into town today.

Jordan is hell-bent on leaving the trail to eat lunch and buy supplies at a town called Newport, Virginia. Daniel is satisfied with the quantity and quality of his food stores. Pearisburg, Virginia, is Daniel's target: a town with hot meals, chilled beer, ice cream, warm showers, and clean sheets. He doesn't want to visit Newport. These guys strike a gentleman's agreement to finish today at War Spur Shelter after they visit Newport.

"Jimmy Doug, you're quiet this morning. What's your plan today?"

"I need to get Buddy off the trail, Jordan. Can you help me with directions to Newport?"

"Do you have a guide book, Jimmy Doug?" Jordan asks.

Daniel glances my way and pulls out *The A.T. Guide* stored in his backpack. He walks over and shows me the book cover.

"I have a trail guide, Jordan. It's different from Daniel's. It's called '*Thru-Hikers' Companion*'. I believe the Appalachian Trail Conservancy publishes this book."

"That's good, Jimmy Doug. These trail guides offer valuable information on and off the trail. Daniel and I keep our books within easy reach. I refer to my guide throughout the day. I'm surprised you haven't used your handbook to plan your exit from the trail."

Jordan speaks the hard truth. Given Buddy's condition this morning, I should stand with these men now, ready to execute a safe plan to deliver my dog to an animal clinic. Daniel politely interrupts Jordan to answer my question before his hiking partner launches into me with harsher remarks.

"Jimmy Doug, follow VA42 to Newport. My guidebook shows the Appalachian Trail cross VA42 a few miles from here," Daniel begins. "Be careful when you reach the first paved road. It's easy to get confused. You cross two paved roads a short distance apart. There is a stream beside the first road intersection. Cross that road. Turn left when you get to the second paved road.

"The town of Newport is eight miles from the second road intersection. When we reach VA42, Jordan and I plan to hitchhike into town to run errands and then catch a ride back to the trail."

Daniel's plan is similar to stories I have read when hikers leave the trail to recover and buy supplies in local communities.

"Will you have trouble getting a ride?" I ask Daniel.

"Jimmy Doug, I've been successful hitchhiking," he responds, as he reaches around the side of his pack. Daniel brings forth a Ukulele and picks a great tune I've never heard. Midway through the chorus, he stops and says:

"I sit on my backpack and play my Ukulele. Before long, a car stops and offers a ride. The strategy works every time." When Daniel finishes his tune, he leads into another melody. It's easy to imagine this artist playing to packed crowds in elegant social settings.

Jordan confirms my impression.

"Daniel is a professional singer and songwriter. Can you believe he wrote the first song you heard on the trail a few days ago?"

I glance at Daniel. He smiles, winks, and keeps playing.

My concern this morning is the casual way Daniel addresses their hitchhiking escapades. I want to believe hitchhiking in rural America is this easy. My experience with back roads is limited to cycling in rural Tennessee and Kentucky. Based on the number of times trucks tried to run me off the road riding my bicycle by myself, rural folks don't care for outsiders who travel their roads.

I was an 18-year-old soldier returning home for Christmas vacation the last time I relied on a stranger for a ride. A winter storm forced the airlines to cancel my connecting flight from Dallas Love Field to Austin, Texas. Back then, I'd walk home before I'd sit in an airport for a day. I spent my last 30 dollars on a taxi ride from the airport terminal to the interstate highway, and then stood in a snow storm wearing my military uniform while carrying a duffle bag. A cute coed stopped for me on IH-35 and delivered me to my parents' front door.

No one fits that hitchhiker's description this morning. We have walked the trail and slept in the woods for several days now. Based on what I see standing before me, if Hollywood is casting a "Hobo Movie", Daniel and Jordan are the first choices. These two characters can hop off a boxcar and star in a movie without makeup or costumes. If these guys catch rides into town appearing this way, Buddy and I will secure transportation. Daniel has his Ukulele and I have my Labrador, Simpson's Buddy-Boy.

The good conversation ends when these two hikers throw their packs on their backs, grab their poles, and walk away from the shelter. Jordan leaves as if he is running a 100-yard dash. He never looks back. Daniel leaves when his hiking partner reaches the incline leading to the trail. Daniel stops 20 yards from the shelter and turns around to wave.

"Jimmy Doug, take care of Buddy today. He is a great dog. I'll see you both again on the trail."

Buddy sits in the shelter's open face and slowly sweeps his tail across the wooden floor as he watches Daniel disappear up the steep incline. When we are alone, my dog settles onto the floor, takes a deep breath, and closes his eyes.

Chapter Ten
Newport, Virginia

I sit with Buddy while he sleeps. My mind covers a myriad of thoughts. People can die when they ingest poison or when they fail to treat severe dehydration. I'm not losing my best friend in the Jefferson National Forest. Phillip is right. Buddy cannot stay here, and he cannot walk out without food and water.

I've learned how to stimulate my dog's appetite. I slip from his side and fix Buddy my breakfast. When the food is prepared, I call my hiking partner to the picnic table.

"Come, Buddy. Help me finish my food. You need carbohydrates to hike this morning."

Buddy-Boy refuses to leave the shelter floor. My Sweet-Boy's message is clear, *"Poppy, my stomach hurts. I'm sorry, but I'm staying at Sarver Hollow today."*

Buddy asked me to stop for the day when we reached the Boy Scout Campsite at Cove Mountain. He suggested we take a rest day at Pickle Branch Shelter. I never considered he'd refuse to leave Sarver Hollow Shelter.

How do I transport my 105-pound Labrador to the animal doctor from this shelter if he can't walk the distance? If we were home, I'd carry him to the truck and drive him to the vet clinic. I'm not in Austin, Texas. I'm standing in a deep hollow by myself, miles from civilization.

"Buddy-Boy, I'm sorry you're having a rough morning. I'll help you get well. Give me a few minutes to map out our best options."

Buddy sighs and settles back on the shelter floor while I collect my thoughts. My dog rests as I examine my map, read my guide book, and finish breakfast. His eyes sadden as I compress the sleeping pallet and return the items to my backpack, then grab the broom and sweep the shelter. Buddy knows I plan to leave Sarver Hollow.

Buddy rises to his forelegs to watch as I set both backpacks in the shelter's back corner and grab a water bottle from its sleeve. I confuse Buddy when I walk empty handed across the wooden floor to sit on the shelter porch ledge by my dog. Buddy moves closer and I stroke his head.

I breathe deeply before I share my plan with Buddy.

"Sweet-Boy, let's call this journey an expensive vacation and head home. I'm leaving our equipment in the shelter and carrying you four miles to the main road. Newport doesn't have a vet clinic. Our best choice is to call Adam when I secure a cellphone connection. Someone will give us a ride to Roanoke. Worst case, I'll find a ride to Pearisburg, VA. When you are stable, we'll drive to Austin. We'll train this winter and start this journey again next spring."

Buddy lifts himself to a sitting position and gazes into my eyes. He's thinking: *"To hell with Newport and Roanoke and Austin, Poppy. You can't carry me out of this hollow. We need to stay here and sleep. I'll eat grass and drink water you boil. I'll recover my energy in a day or two. You'll see."*

"Buddy-Boy, we do not know what you've swallowed in the last three days, and I can't help you if your condition worsens. I will not stay here and watch you die in my arms. I can and will carry you to the main road, Sweet-Boy."

Buddy's heard enough. He rises to his feet, gingerly walks to the corner where I stacked our packs and waits for me to place his pack on his back. Buddy is strong-willed. No one is carrying Buddy today.

The hardest work we face today is the climb from this hollow to the Appalachian Trail. We need to ascend 300 feet over a short distance to reach the dirt path and begin our hiking day. We walk up the steep incline we descended in the pouring rain last evening; same path, two distinct experiences. I braked with feet, ankles, knees, and hips; preventing falls by balancing with my hiking poles. Now, I pull my poles with shoulders and back, and scale this incline by pushing my body with the same feet, ankles, knees, and hips. My energy stores immediately deplete. This climb will finish Buddy.

When I hit the notorious "wall" running marathons, my spirit removes me from my immediate situation. I survive the physical and mental punishment for miles in a surreal zone until the ordeal ends. The best medicine for Buddy might be a playful distraction.

"Hey Buddy, the Sarver Hollow footpath is interesting—going downhill is risky. Climbing uphill is painful. Let's hike the whole Appalachian Trail traveling southbound, then retrace our steps heading northbound. When we finish both journeys, I'll buy you a puppy to play with in the yard. Once you wear him out, you can lie beside me in our office and help me write a book describing the nuances we discover between the northbound and southbound adventures. What do you say, partner?"

I take a few steps before I'm aware Buddy's dog tags have stopped jingling. As I pivot on the steep incline, I see Buddy standing still, legs locked solid. He's adopted his new "I refuse to move until you stop your crazy antics" pose. Laughter pours from my gut across Sarver Hollow as I move downhill to my friend.

"Buddy-Boy, I'm kidding. I won't buy you a puppy."

Buddy takes on a sterner disposition and sits his butt on the incline. I laugh harder and louder.

"Buddy, I'm playing with you," I say, tugging on his collar, and giving him a big hug.

We are adapting to our new environment. If I attempted to show this affection on this downhill slope on day one, we'd have fallen to the incline's bottom. Today, we love each other and laugh.

Playtime ends once Buddy reaches out a front paw to get my attention. When I shake his paw, my dog shares his thoughts: *"Poppy, please don't tease me today. I'll get to the main road. Be patient and stop the jokes."*

"I'm sorry, Buddy. You are a good dog. Relax and take your time. Here's the truth: I may have the will, the time, and the finances to finish such an undertaking myself, but I am positive I do not have the physical wherewithal. You know my right foot toes stopped working in Kansas. I suffered leg pain every time I tried to run with speed for distance in Mobile, Alabama, this summer. You've seen me fall this first week on the trail. Something is affecting my leg strength, balance, and agility. We will be lucky to finish half—let alone complete this whole journey by ourselves, one time."

Buddy accepts my apology. He rises and continues to follow me up the incline at his pace. As usual, I am lost in deep thought when the side trail intersects with the Appalachian Trail. Thank goodness, the intersection is a 'T', or I'd walk by the direction sign I missed yesterday in the rain. I stop today and admire the letters carved in the wood waiting for Buddy to come up beside me: "3.9 miles to VA42."

My Sweet-Boy suffers, but he's not finished. There is fire in his eyes. Will drives my dog this morning. No one carries Buddy. He is here to guide and protect me.

"Buddy, it's time for a serious conversation. I am taking your pack and carrying it for you to the main road. I cannot pack your load next week. Backpackers shoulder their weight in the backcountry. Do you understand?"

Buddy grasps the message I intend to convey with my words. I can see it in his eyes and his body language. He thinks he has disappointed me. His thought is farthest from the truth. I am very proud of my dog. He made a mistake this week he needs to fix; same as the errors I made which I will eliminate if we plan to stay on the trail.

I sit on the dirt path and take off Buddy's pack. The trail is a good place to sit, given the lack of human foot traffic. Buddy stands looking me straight in the face while I stroke his ears and neck.

"Buddy, if the doctor lets you return to the trail next week, we must both change our behavior. You must stop drinking every form of liquid you walk by during the day. The putrid stuff has made you sick. If you don't stop drinking everything in sight, you'll get sick, again. Next time, the veterinarian will make me send you back to Texas. You know I can't make it out here without you."

When I finish with his pep-talk, Buddy's eyes sparkle. He opens his mouth and lets his tongue hang from the side. Buddy gets what I am saying. I hope I've regained a level of his confidence.

"My turn, Buddy," I continue. "You know I daydream—I lose myself in deep thought. Your job is keep us on the right path. Will you help me watch for the white blazes and trail signs? If we go 500 yards without seeing a trail marker, will you please make sure we stop and go back until we find one?"

Buddy stares in disbelief.

"Poppy, what do you think I have been trying to do for you this whole week? Pops, let's talk roles again: you are Poppy, and I am your dog. I'll give my best to keep you safe moving in the right direction. You give your best to take care of us. Now, snap to it and pay attention. This is dangerous business and I want to get home to our family in one piece, someday."

Buddy's right. I call my daughter, Lacey, when I gain cell phone coverage a mile up the trail. When we finish chatting, I call Reece. My perspective improves when I finish talking to them. I may walk with Buddy in solitude, but I am not alone. Both women express concern when they hear Buddy is suffering. Austin is 1,276 miles from Newport, Virginia. The best my family can offer today is a shared hope Buddy is sick with flu symptoms.

When I finish calling my family, I call my friends in Roanoke. Roanoke is 51 miles from Newport, Virginia. When I describe Buddy's symptoms, Maye agrees to meet us after work in Newport, on VA42.

"Jimmy Doug, I'm studying a map. I see a convenience store on the east side of Newport. I can pick you up at the store."

"Maye, we will try to reach the store. Given our stamina, you will find us waiting on the west side of town where VA42 intersects with the Appalachian Trail. Look for a hobo sitting beside a light gray Labrador."

"Buddy is white, Jimmy Doug. What happened to Buddy-Boy?"

"It's a good story, Maye. I'll tell you when I see you."

"How are your feet, Jimmy Doug?" Adam asks.

"The boots tore both my feet to hell, Doctor. The blisters may be infected."

"I told you to buy new boots and socks!"

"Don't worry, Adam. The Appalachian Trail's delivered a proper spanking for the oversight. Boots and socks are one of many mistakes I made preparing for this venture. I'll see you both in a few hours."

"Jimmy Doug, take care of Buddy. I'll find you on the west side of Newport," Maye promises.

I'm relieved we aren't depending on my thumb for a ride to Pearisburg, Virginia, to find a veterinarian. "Thank you for coming to get us on short notice, Maye."

"No problem, Jimmy Doug. We'll get Buddy the care he needs and get you patched and back on the trail."

I've carried Buddy's equipment by hand, shifting his kit from arm to arm. When we finish with our calls, I lash his pack to the top of my backpack. This simple change is helpful. More importantly, it's easier walking toward someone rather than something.

We follow Sinking Creek Mountain's undulating ridgeline for 1.5 miles, before we descend the mountain's backside—920 feet to arrive near a massive oak tree named '*Keffer Oak*'. The guide book says the tree is over 18 feet around and its age is estimated at 300 years old.

Keffer Oak impresses me the same way the Grand Canyon moves me. This tree stands without peer after three centuries; two tenths of a mile north of VA630. I wonder why nature set this natural phenomenon apart to live today.

We are alone; there are no crowds with cameras, no commercial buildings sharing limited space, and no monument memorializing this living accomplishment. I take off the packs, sit on the ground, and lean against this magnificent oak to absorb its energy. The Sarver Family comes to my mind. How often did a Sarver sit in my place to rest, meditate, court a neighbor, close an act of commerce, or play with siblings and friends? How many strangers have sat where I sit and leaned against this tree? Imagine the stories this silent participant could share if asked.

"Hey Buddy, come sit with me," I ask, as I pat the ground by my side. "Rest your back against the tree trunk. The shade this tree provides is comforting. Come, Sweet-Boy."

Buddy rests on his haunches and scratches my pants once he's settled by my side.

"Are you hungry, Buddy-Boy? Let's see what's stored in this pocket," I say, as I reach into my side pouch and pull out Buddy's favorite candy bar.

I smile with relief watching my dog's countenance change once I unwrap his Snickers. My Labrador doesn't refuse this treat. He eats the high-energy candy in two bites. We share another energy bar, one small bite at a time, before we split a water bottle mixed with electrolytes.

The breeze that blows across our bodies is relaxing under Keffer Oak's protective shade. Before long, I'm asleep. I wake with a jerk when my chin bumps my chest. Buddy sleeps soundly. He needs to rest, but we can't afford a nap this morning. I nudge my dog's side and scratch his back to get his attention.

"Buddy, open your eyes. Let's sit and relax with Keffer Oak a few minutes, then get to VA42 to catch our ride to Roanoke with Maye."

My Labrador rolls on his side and lies his head on my leg. My eyes close and we are fast asleep under a 300-year-old oak tree planted a short walk from a stream of fast moving water. I am exhausted—in body, mind, and in spirit. I must stay in deep stages of NREM sleep.

When I waken, I am disoriented until I sense the bark of the Keffer Oak imprinted in my back. How long have I slept? My wristwatch says I slept for two hours under this shady tree. Without thinking, I reach over to pat Buddy. He is right beside me with his back touching the big oak. I wonder if he dreamed.

"Sweet-Boy, wake up. We've slept two hours. If we hurry, we can still meet Maye in Newport."

We hustle under Jefferson National Forest tree cover to the VA42 intersection with a pace resembling that of two old men pounded by nature for four straight days.

I'm surprised when we arrive at a paved road with a swollen creek spilling water over its bank to our right within 30 minutes. Buddy moves into the fast-moving water to quench his thirst, while I drink my second bottle then refill both containers. It's fun watching my dog play in the creek. Maybe heavy run-off moving through Sinking Creek is nature's promise our fight with Central Virginia's drought is concluded.

When Buddy scales the creek embankment and returns to my side, we head west toward Newport on a smooth asphalt road with no traffic. A small farm catches my eye as we pass the property on our left. I envy the man standing by a tractor. The farmer is clean. He seems at peace living in the world he's created. I wave a greeting without expecting a response.

"Where are you boys headed on Northside Road with that pack on your back?" the farmer asks with a friendly tone.

"My dog needs medical attention, sir. I'm taking him to Newport," I answer, hoping this man will offer us a ride to town.

"Let's see, I guess this road will take you to Newport in a roundabout way. You'll be better off returning to the trailhead by the bridge and heading south on the Appalachian Trail, till you hit VA42."

"Thank you, sir. I'll take your advice."

"No problem. Good luck with your dog. I'm headed to the house to eat lunch." And with those words, the landowner turns his back, waves goodbye, and walks across his yard to enjoy a mid-day meal.

Buddy and I watch the man enter his home then turn back to connect with the Appalachian Trail. My dog walks beside me on the open road.

"Poppy, is the farmer a trail angel? He didn't offer help; no water, food, shelter, or transportation."

"Buddy, we didn't need material help. We needed information. He offered a greater gift: dignity. He saved us from another lost in the woods experience."

Chapter Eleven
Newcomers

I stick out my thumb, smile, and wave as cars pass by on VA42. No luck. Drivers wave at Buddy, but no one will contaminate their vehicle sharing a ride with a dirty dog and a smelly man.

"I guess we need a Ukulele, Buddy-Boy."

Maye is a welcomed sight. She can't hide her concern behind a friendly greeting.

"My, oh my, Jimmy Doug. Your appearance is distinctive."

"Thanks, Maye. We've experienced better days," I say, returning her friendly smile.

"Come here, Buddy-Boy. You need your belly scratched."

Buddy loves Maye. He comes to her on command and submits to her brief, but thorough, roadside physical examination. When she finishes Buddy's check-up, she plays with her pal and then she visits me.

"Jimmy Doug, you and your dog are a mess. You were smart to leave the trail. Buddy's dehydrated and his gut is painful. I can't treat him. With your permission, I suggest we take him to a veterinary clinic in Roanoke."

"You're the family doctor, ma'am," I answer, as I help load Buddy into the SUV's cargo area, then lay our equipment in the back seat.

Maye drives straight to a storefront veterinary clinic that caters to house pets. The animal doctor is confused when she sees Buddy and me. I doubt she's ever seen a man and animal present in our condition in her exam room. Maye presents her medical credentials to the veterinarian and explains to the doctor Buddy-Boy is not a pet; he is a trained endurance athlete. Buddy has walked step for step with me on the Appalachian Trail.

The doctor's preliminary diagnosis is severe dehydration. She completes a full blood work-up, gives Buddy IV fluids, and treats him for a 'stomach bug'. The blood work does not suggest poison. This is the best news I can hope to hear today.

"Mr. Simpson, Buddy is a remarkable animal. I can't stop him from following you on this journey. He will make his own decision whether he returns to the Appalachian Trail after resting."

"I agree, Doctor. Thank you very much."

Maye leaves the PetSmart parking lot and drives me to Gander Mountain to buy Keen waterproof hiking boots and wool socks, then delivers me to the hospital to see Adam. When we pull into the driveway at the hospital's main entrance, I see a mild-mannered male setting on a bench. He is wearing a suit with a bow tie and round, rimless glasses. It's Adam in his "Clark Kent" physician's outfit.

"Jimmy Doug, Adam set up the GPS tracking tool I exchanged for you while you walked the trail this week. 'Spot' is the device's name. Please act surprised when we get to his office."

Spot is a good tool I am glad I can carry to call for help in an emergency. Unlike my cell phone, Spot transmits by satellite, not through the cellphone tower. When I push a button on the device's face, Spot signals a satellite. The satellite forwards a canned message to designated email accounts with specific GPS coordinates marking my location on computer maps recipients can follow on the internet.

Jeff Zwiener is my marathon running partner. Jeff believes in the device. He advised me to carry Spot on this trip. He told me, "When a disaster occurs, a GPS tracking device alerts people you are in big trouble. Designated people will guide rescue teams to deliver prompt, professional aid, based on your GPS coordinates."

Jeff wrote me in one of many encouraging emails:

"Doug, if you carry Spot, the guys and I will get you to safety. 'Blackhawk-Down' is code for Doug's in trouble."

Spot did not make it to my backpack the first morning. Buddy and I walked with limited ability to contact the world the first week. I am indebted to Adam for using his family time to shop for Spot and make it ready for use next week.

Adam examines my feet when we arrive at his office. He smiles when he sees how I applied superglue to open wounds and dead toe nails.

"Nice job, Jimmy Doug. No sign of infection in either foot. I will need a surgical assistant on the next medical humanitarian trip. Keep practicing with the superglue and I will call you."

"Yes, sir," I respond with enthusiasm. Adam's playing with me today, but working beside physicians and nurses in underprivileged areas is a dream opportunity.

Adam is pleased I purchased a new pair of lightweight hiking boots. He insisted I buy these boots and new socks before I left for the trail. I'm sure he wants to tease me, but he doesn't.

Adam releases me back to Maye's care with these instructions:

"Jimmy Doug, promise me you will be careful, and buy more band aids and superglue."

Maye invites us to share her home while Buddy recovers. After a shower, a home cooked meal, and good conversation shared over a bottle of Trump Winery Cabernet, I head to bed, where I sleep next to Buddy off and on for two days.

Maye and her roommate care for Buddy while I sleep. They buy my dog a large foam pad and make him a bed. He hydrates, eats soup and wet dog food, and takes his medication. The first time I rollover to check on Buddy, he's lying prone on a mattress with a sheet and a pillow. I shake my head. Maye has spoiled Buddy for life. He'll never go back with me to the Appalachian Trail.

Buddy is sore but regaining his strength. His medication helps. Whatever ailed him at Sarver Hollow has subsided by Saturday afternoon. We walk to a park near Maye's home that evening, stopping on a rise overlooking a small pond filled with ducks and geese. We stand together for minutes with our own thoughts. I'm returning to the trail tomorrow morning. It's time for Buddy to make his own decision.

"Buddy, I've packed and I'm heading back to the trail tomorrow. Pearisburg, Virginia to Atkins, Virginia is a 90 mile walk. We can hike that distance in seven days. What do you say, Simpson's Buddy-Boy? You have nice accommodation at Maye's. I'll understand if you decide to stay here. I've packed both our backpacks. If you want to return to the Appalachian Trail with me, I've lightened your backpack."

Buddy moves closer and slides his torso against my hand until it rests on his sweet-spot as if to say, *"I go where you go, Poppy. I'll be fine."*

I scratch his back where his hip muscles join his back. When Buddy is ready, we walk back to Maye's at a good pace.

Chapter Twelve
Pearisburg, Virginia

My father loves golf. He plays to win. I love playing golf with my father. There's a big difference. I pay my green fee to spend special time with my dad. When I put a golf club in my hand, I spray my drive from the tee box right, left, or dribble the golf ball into the fairway. My father keeps score. He's a generous man. Dad ignores my first stroke when he tallies my score. He grants me a mulligan and I take my second shot beside my father's first shot. The Appalachian Trail does not grant mulligans.

When I was in elementary school, the National Football League kicked off its new season with an exhibition game. The opponents were the reigning NFL championship team and a group of collegiate all-stars. I loved to watch the game on television with my cousins. The best team in the world played newcomers; great young athletes with no professional experience and no team loyalty. The action was entertaining when the score wasn't close. Players played professional football. Final scores didn't matter.

This NFL kick-off game reminds me of my first week on the Appalachian Trail. Buddy and I are newcomers: good athletes with no practical experience; facing challenging terrain in hot, dry conditions.

We made mistakes during the first week. We both paid a physical price for those errors. The trail kicked us hard. We kept our composure and did not quit walking. I believe we met the first week standard; we survived. We gave our best effort and enjoyed everything Nature placed in our path. The first week is history. It's time to apply what we learned.

Buddy and I wake Sunday morning in Roanoke, ready for a fresh start. We are clean, rested, hydrated, and we understand the challenge we face. Buddy-Boy makes sure I do not leave him behind when I return to the Jefferson National Forest. He walks outside and stations himself beside Maye's vehicle while I fill water bottles and organize our equipment to leave.

The drive from Roanoke to Pearisburg is brief. Maye drives one hour and covers a distance I'd hike mountains five days to achieve the same result. She asks me for directions once we cross New River on US460 and arrive at Pearisburg, Virginia, early Sunday afternoon.

"I'm not positive where the trailhead intersects in Pearisburg, Maye. The *Thru-Hikers' Companion* map is vague. The Appalachian Trail crosses a residential street near a Dairy Queen on main street."

"Why does a wilderness trail cross through a neighborhood, Jimmy Doug?"

"Beats me, Maye. The location strikes me as odd, but I'm in no position to second guess trail-maker nuances. If I hiked into Pearisburg, I'd be happy to step off the trail and order a DQ Blizzard."

Maye turns onto Main Street and drives straight to the Dairy Queen. I order three ice cream cones and ask the young lady taking orders from the outside window for directions to the trailhead.

"Mister, I wish I could help you, but I've never heard an Appalachian Trail mentioned."

"No problem," I say to Buddy. I find a bench to sit on outside the store. We watch traffic move in and out of a gas station parking lot while we finish our ice cream cones. Once I see a man drop to the ground from a pickup, wearing boots and a ballcap. I believe we have found someone who can help us with directions.

When I hear this man's dialect, I swear I'm in Southern Alabama or Middle Tennessee. This fella has a perfect southern drawl. He is familiar with the neighborhood trailhead leading to the Appalachian Trail. He's surprised we are passing through Pearisburg this late in the season. The friendly man pumps gas into his truck and gives us directions.

"Jimmy Doug, this street is Johnston Avenue, and that street is Morris Avenue. Morris Avenue changes its name to Cross Avenue. Cross Avenue intersects with the footpath. Southbound hikers enter the thick bushes by the sign and head in this direction." The local man guides me by pointing his finger in a direction I assume leads south.

The man is right. When we arrive at the Cross Avenue Trailhead, we stare at a thick vegetation wall. I see the white blaze marking the trail, but I can't find a path from the street.

Maye stares from the driver seat through my passenger window at the jungle we need to penetrate.

"Jimmy Doug, do you trust the man at the convenience store?"

"Why not, Maye? What does he have to gain from misleading me? This is the footpath. Can you see the trail sign?" I say, pointing to the marking.

"Okay, I believe you, Jimmy Doug. Call it intuition, but I sense trouble."

I smile, reach over the SUV's console, and hug Maye goodbye. When we release each other, I brush my fingers across her face to chase away her tears.

"We'll be fine, Maye. Thank you for caring. Buddy and I start back today because you lent your strength to us when we were weakest. Remember we agreed, no worries."

Maye shares a wicked smile as my words register with her, then she speaks her truth:

"Right, Jimmy Doug. You are so full of yourself. No worries. Remember who picked you up on VA42 and drove Buddy straight to the animal doctor? Who nursed that sweet-boy while you slept for two days? Now, he's back on the trail with you. Don't be ridiculous—no worries."

I can't reason with Maye, so I don't try. She has a valid concern. The problem is, Buddy decides for himself.

"Jimmy Doug, when will you arrive in Atkins, Virginia?"

"If the hike goes as planned, we reach Atkins Saturday afternoon."

"Okay, we have a date. I'll meet you in Atkins Saturday afternoon. I want to make sure you are both fit before Buddy starts another week."

"Thanks, Maye. We'll work to make Saturday in Atkins a reality."

When I place our packs on our backs, Maye takes our picture, then embraces Buddy. She whispers private words to my Labrador, then speaks louder for my ears.

"Buddy-Boy, please protect this old fool from himself this week."

Buddy licks Maye's cheek, then glances my way and wags his tail. Maye, you need not worry.

When the SUV's hazard lights stop flashing and Maye disappears around a bend, I turn my attention to the trailhead and Buddy.

"Where is the footpath, Buddy?" I ask, expecting Buddy to move forward.

My dog stands still and looks left. I follow Buddy-Boy's eyes with my own. I see a pleasant lady push a lawnmower across a well-maintained yard. The lady waves and smiles when she has my attention. I smile and wave to the friendly homeowner, then turn my back without speaking, and force myself into the dense vegetation.

Tall weeds and thick brush cover the walking space. When I look straight to the ground, I glimpse the footpath through the dense foliage. Buddy-Boy stays close and uses my body as a shield. We stop several times in a 10-minute span to free both packs from tangled plant life.

I'm disappointed at the trail's condition. I wish I had a machete to clean up the passageway. Disappointment turns to frustration, which evolves to anger, then resentment when I crawl to navigate the footpath.

This is pathetic. Trail volunteers work across obscure miles at personal expense to protect the Appalachian Trail's integrity. This isn't a dense forest shared with spirits, it's 0.35-miles of ground in a Pearisburg, Virginia-neighborhood. People drive by the trailhead every day. No one tends to this national treasure when Buddy and I walk this town's streets. The Appalachian Trail and its visitors deserve better.

When we exit the dense foliage, we return to a maze of concrete we traveled by car to reach Pearisburg and find the Dairy Queen.

"Come here, Buddy," I say, as we cross New River on a walkway paralleling the Senator Schumacher Bridge. "Check out the water flow in this river. Maybe rain quenched the drought while we slept this weekend."

Buddy is pleased. He moves ahead until we leave the bridge and track white blaze markers painted on concrete barriers and asphalt road surface that lead us to a tranquil forest. We make excellent time on this wilderness trail.

After five miles into today's walk, I clamber over a fallen tree blocking the footpath and notice two thru-hikers heading our way. These men hike with a purpose, moving at an athletic pace. Once we meet face-to-face, I learn these thru-hikers are a father and son team from Atlanta, Georgia. The father is my age. The son is a software engineer who quit his job to share this journey with his dad. They hustle this afternoon to meet the father's wife and the son's mother in Pearisburg. This is Mom's third trip to join her men on their journey.

The hikers introduce themselves by their trail names: Newt and Kermit. When they ask my trail name, I am stumped. A trail name isn't important when you walk in solitude. I want to introduce myself as Poppy but choose Jimmy Doug.

"My trail name is Jimmy Doug, and this dog is my hiking partner, Simpson's Buddy-Boy."

"Well, it's nice to meet you both, Jimmy Doug and Buddy-Boy. Forgive me Jimmy Doug, but I'm wondering if your trail name should be 'Wrong Way', Newt asks with a smile.

I don't get the joke, but it doesn't matter. I enjoy laughing at myself when the humor is presented in a fun way.

"Wrong Way is an interesting name, Newt. Why do you suggest it?"

"The name fits your location, Wrong Way," Kermit responds for his father. He wears a similar smile on his face. "Didn't you tell us you are a southbound hiker? We are southbound hikers. You just crossed the West Virginia State Line. Jimmy Doug, you and Buddy are walking in the wrong direction. You are headed back to Roanoke instead of walking to Springer Mountain."

I laugh aloud. My mistake is funny. No—it's hilarious. I hope Buddy sees the humor in our predicament. Poor Buddy, the name Wrong Way fits me perfect.

Jordan taught me an unspoken lesson the night I offered him water at Sarver Hollow Shelter. Jordan was respectful, but he did not trust my information. He accepted my gift, but still boiled the water before he filled his water containers. I trusted the local man who drove the jacked-up truck without pulling out a map to verify the directions he offered. The prankster at the gas station must have seen me coming a mile away. I'll bet he has a big time at my expense around the supper table, and a bigger time at the local beer joint tonight.

What can I say or do? I laugh, shake my head, tip my hat to the friendly man at the gas station, and emphasize to Newt and Kermit:

"My trail name is: Jimmy Doug."

"Yes, Wrong Way, your trail name is Jimmy Doug," Newt responds with a light tone added to his strong Georgia accent. "We appreciate the fact you walked out to West Virginia to escort us into town. Mighty generous of you."

With this final taunt launched my way, we laugh again, then get to the business of walking to Pearisburg, Virginia. Buddy and I gain quality experience hiking with these seasoned backcountry travelers. The pace they move, and the way they manage their backpack and hiking poles is informative. The stories they share during our brief time together are well worth the extra miles we walk today.

I describe the jungle they face as we travel across the Senator Schumate Bridge. Kermit reaches for his map as I describe crawling sections to penetrate the vegetation.

Kermit chimes in when I finish my story.

"Jimmy Doug, a street named 'Lane' intersects with Main Street. Since you've completed this section, you can follow Lane Street to Cross Avenue to avoid the hassle. Dad and I are purists. We've committed to walk every step on the Appalachian Trail footpath, so we'll stay with the footpath to reach Cross Avenue."

Buddy and I slow our pace once we decide to take a different route into Pearisburg. The Georgia boys pause long enough to leave with friendly words.

"Buddy-Boy, you are an elite animal. I'm glad I can say I walked with a backcountry walker of your quality."

Buddy impresses everyone when he moves to face Newt, sits, and then extends a paw to shake his hand. My Labrador is a smart companion and a class act.

"Jimmy Doug, take care. I hope we see you on the trail. We can compare notes on the jungle experience."

My dog and I return to Cross Avenue's neighborhood in the late afternoon. We've just walked 10-unplanned-miles. The temperature is pleasant, and the sky is bright blue. It's nice to see Buddy energized. We made the right decision leaving the trail to regroup and receive medical attention. Our hike to meet Kermit and Newt was a good test.

If the northbound trail connects to Cross Avenue, the southbound trail is close. When we return to the northbound trailhead, I scan the neighborhood for a dirt path. I see a residential street fronting well-kept homes with landscaped lawns. I cannot find a dirt path, a white blaze, or a wooden sign marking the southbound trailhead. This is a certainty; the Appalachian Trail does not end in this neighborhood in Pearisburg, Virginia.

"Where is the trail, Buddy-Boy?" I ask in frustration. Buddy leads, and I follow as he walks to the lawn the lady mowed earlier in the day. Sure enough, white paint sits on a tree standing in her side yard.

"You were right, Buddy. The Appalachian Trail existed to our left when I forced us into the dense vegetation."

This woman enjoys her yard. Flowers and healthy shrubs fill the property. Well-groomed grass covers the Appalachian Trail's dirt path. As Buddy and I walk over her lawn, she steps onto her front porch and smiles, again. I'm disappointed she doesn't speak before she returns to the comfort of her home. I'd hoped she stepped outside to invite us to join her for supper.

We leave Cross Avenue's neighborhood and climb Pearis Mountain's spine for an hour before we cross Mercy Branch, a stream running below Angel's Rest's southern face. Angel's Rest is a popular day hike offered to anyone ready to climb 1,650-feet over 1.5-miles to sit on a boulder and look over New River.

Flat ground stands above running water a short distance from the stream. We stop to hydrate, and I fill my water bottles before we climb the rise to reach a small plateau separating the stream climb from the next incline. The forest is evening gray. A large tree trunk rests on flat ground beside the trail. Common sense tells me, *bivouac here tonight.*

"Buddy, we can't reach Doc's Knob Shelter before dark. This flat ground is a gift. Let's stay here, tonight."

Buddy agrees with my decision. He knows the routine. Once I take his pack, he heads downhill to the stream and waits while I fill the cooking pot. We finish our chores and are asleep on the ground next to the log before the forest turns night gray.

I wake once in the wee hours. Brilliant specks of light in the night sky and a bright moon illuminate our mountain home. The air is cool and damp. Buddy's tucked his head under my rain cover. He deserves better. I lift the tarp and move closer to the log we use for protection. Buddy slides beside me, jamming me between the tree and himself.

"Buddy, help yourself to the air mattress," I whisper, as I wiggle in my sleeping bag liner to create a fraction more space for myself.

Chapter Thirteen
Doc's Knob Shelter

Pearis Mountain tests us today. I've never walked a roller-coaster track. The ridgeline we hike for 2.5-miles might be comparable. The footpath climbs 425-feet and falls 603-feet, then turns hard right and drops straight down the mountainside for a short distance to a path the trail makers carved into Pearis Mountain's side. We turn hard left onto the narrow passageway and cut across the mountain's face for another 3.5-miles before we drop 456-feet to ascend another 790-feet to complete the hiking day.

Comfortable temperatures and plentiful water resources make a difficult climb bearable. Buddy and I are strong when we reach the wooden sign announcing our arrival at Doc's Knob Shelter.

"Nice job, Buddy-Boy. Shall we stop for the day? We can't reach the next shelter before dusk. We can stay here or hike until sunset and sleep on the ground. Doc's Knob has water and an outhouse. Your choice: roof or ground?"

My dog strides to the shelter and waits for me to remove his pack. Buddy picks roof.

Doc's Knob Shelter is a typical three-walled building with an open front. The shelter has a single floor built to sleep eight people. Running water is accessible, and the outhouse is convenient to the shelter and the trail.

The building is empty this afternoon. I half expect to see Kermit and Newt before we fall asleep. Daniel and Jordan surprise me when they enter the shelter grounds this afternoon. We met these southbound thru-hikers at Sarver Hollow Shelter. Both men are agitated when they greet us. They remove their equipment and place it on the picnic table before I can say:

"Hello, how was the hiking day?"

Daniel is fast. Jordan is quicker. I laugh when I see Jordan unbuckle his pants while he hops cross-legged to the outhouse. Based on body language, I'm not betting Daniel survives with clean pants if he waits long for Jordan to finish his business. When the privy door opens, Daniel executes his version of the cross-legged hop and disappears into quarters I'm happy to vacate right now.

I appreciate picnic tables placed outside shelters. The table top and benches are friendly territory for strangers to gather as one. The surface is comfortable as a living room recliner after a day walking this terrain. When the boys' grand entrance has concluded, everyone settles around the picnic table to relax before we start our evening routine.

"Jordan, did you have luck hitchhiking to Newport on the main road?"

"Not a problem, Jimmy Doug. Daniel pulled out the Ukulele. A local lady offered us a ride within 10-minutes. She invited us to her home, allowed us to shower, fed us lunch, entertained us, drove us to the store, and brought us back to the trailhead."

"Impressive," I say, looking to Daniel to add to this story.

He nods his head in agreement and smiles.

Young, fearless, and lucky is how I gauge my shelter mates this evening.

Daniel gives Buddy a good head rub then says:

"Buddy's strong, Jimmy Doug. I assume you found your way to an animal doctor?"

Before I respond, Kermit blows into the camp ground. He drops his pack on the picnic table and heads for the outhouse with a smile and wave. When Kermit exits the privy, his father arrives. If Newt could enter the outhouse and drop his load with his equipment on, he'd do it today.

I'm grateful I didn't need to pinch my butt cheeks and hope for the best when I walked the roller-coaster from Pearisburg to Doc's Knob Shelter. This whole experience is comical, especially for a newcomer standing with seasoned hikers.

Backpackers carry food a body requires to balance calories consumed with calories burned in a day. A hot meal in the woods differs from a home-cooked meal. Hot means boiled water added to prepackaged food. Long distance walkers compensate by consuming rich food and strong beverages when they arrive at a store or restaurant.

When I reach a town, my mind convinces my body it's starving. I'm not hungry. I'm craving comfort food and drinks. Jordan and Daniel indulged their cravings and paid the price today. Newt and Kermit left the shelter before I asked Newt if walking the wrong-way is the same as making the wrong choice. The Georgia boys head for 'Woods Hole Hostel as soon as Newt finishes his business in the privy. I'm not sure if they wanted to be pampered another night, or they wanted to avoid being crammed into this shelter with three guys and my big dog.

Daniel and I connected the first night at Sarver Hollow Shelter. He is younger than my son and son-in-law, but he has their spirit. My boys are strong, intelligent men with good work ethics, a kind and generous countenance, and tender hearts.

Daniel is a natural entertainer. He's in a playful mood tonight. This showman concocts a whooper narrative for my amusement and his entertainment. The story line is his education and professional experience. There is no reason for me to disbelieve Daniel's life account. If he says he attended Ivy League Schools to earn undergraduate and law degrees, then he did. If Daniel tells me that he is taking a break on the Appalachian Trail before he begins medical school at a different Ivy League School, then he is.

Who knows, Daniel may be a savant? I've known individuals with towering intellects, but never hung around one who skips baths for days and sleeps in a bag lying on a plank floor in the woods. Maybe Daniel is my first.

Buddy and I lie back on the shelter floor while Daniel and Jordan collaborate to spin their tale from the picnic table bench. When Daniel finishes the narrative, I engage him in conversation, adding small amounts of my life story. I share a brief description of why I walk this trail. When I finish, Daniel knows he needs a different story.

I'm grateful Daniel feels comfortable with me and Buddy. When he climbs into his sleeping bag across the shelter, he opens his heart to us.

"Jimmy Doug, I couldn't unplug back home. My phone demanded my attention. My time belonged to everyone but me.

Everywhere I turned, people told me what I was doing wrong. They offered unsolicited advice on how I should live my life, then demanded, instead of requested, my help to fulfill their obligations. Fresh air was hard to find at home.

"I've seen so many adults lose connection with their children. Stress cripples the adult world. Moms and dads flame out before their families; abusing alcohol and drugs and engaging in serial marriages.

"Jimmy Doug, I refuse to follow this pattern when I am a man living before my children. When I step into the adult world full-time, I want to know I am choosing the best direction. I need to be confident in my choices when I devote money and time to finish my higher education, choose a career, and find a life partner.

"I started my hike in New Jersey. Trust me, the Appalachian Trail is a mighty challenge. I accept hardship to enjoy silence. I've unplugged from my world to think without distraction or interference. When I know me and what I want, I will leave the wilderness; prepared to engage the next phase of life."

I close my eyes and see my son's face while I listen to this young man from New Jersey. Daniel's account is James' narrative. A few years ago, our family flew to New York to enroll James at the United States Military Academy in West Point, New York. Our son worked hard in the classroom and on the baseball field to earn his opportunity.

"Are you ready for this challenge, James?" I asked my boy, standing outside the West Point Baseball Complex. His adrenaline was running hard. He was excited; surrounded by new teammates. Every ballplayer was a leader at West Point. My son played the catcher position. Catchers lead leaders. James was playing his part this morning. When the baseball coach arrived to meet with his new players, our son walked away from his mother and me without answering my question.

I live this pivotal moment for my son through my dream for my son. The fact James is leaving us is not real. He is still our boy; a strapping baseball player with long hair and an unlimited future. Our son returns to us for a final goodbye later in the afternoon. He marches as a soldier, wearing military clothing and a shaved head. My dream is now my son's reality. Our son is no longer our boy. James is our child, and he is his own man attempting to fulfill his father's wishes. The day is poignant.

Reece and I raised James to leave the nest, find his path to adulthood, and then make his own mark on his sphere of influence. He venerated me by accepting this prestigious opportunity. He honored himself by walking away from West Point his first semester to find his own way, his way.

Before James left the United States Military Academy, he finished the seven-week Cadet Basic Training Course and established himself as a valued member of Army's varsity baseball team. He proved to himself he had the gameness to compete in this environment. I'm grateful James possessed the moxie to standup for himself before he committed to live my dream for him.

A week after the 2004 Madrid train bombings killed 191-people and injured over 1,800-more-victims, James gathered his life savings and his passport. He purchased an airline ticket and flew alone to Madrid. He spent six months by himself, living out of a backpack and embracing the culture offered in this Spanish speaking country.

Fathering is a tough business. What is the best way for me to promote free thinking, encourage risk taking, and value social service? How do I teach independence and self-reliance and still protect my children's future from thoughtless behavior and the avaricious influences that surround them? When do I nurture, encourage, mentor, guide, lead or become a protective obstacle?

The way I make choices and conduct my personal life, matters. When I make a parenting mistake, I suffer remorse and fix my error. My family isn't as lucky. James and Lacey live with the predicament my decision or behavior creates.

My mistake this time: status. I am enthralled with future opportunities the degree and military commitment can yield for my son and the prestige a West Point Appointment provides my entire family. Is my rational wrong? No, not if I'm the person committing to the task.

My lesson is learned: mentor others to make the best decisions for themselves. They live with the choice, not me.

Headlamps pierce the darkness when I finish these thoughts. Both men are studying their trail guides. Forest sounds mingle with shelter silence, in a quiet rhythm that rocks me to the first stage of sleep while Buddy-Boy rests against my side.

Daniel breaks the stillness.

"Jimmy Doug, are you awake? Did I tell you my dad and uncle are meeting me in Atkins, Virginia on Friday? I promised them we'd spend Saturday night at Knot Maul Branch Shelter, and then hike back to Atkins on Sunday."

"What a gift, Daniel. You guide your father. Dad will have the chance to see you as an equal on this testing ground. He will be proud."

I wish I could trade places with Daniel's father and Jordan's father tonight. I sense the love and respect both hold for their parents—even more for their siblings. Both families have raised good sons.

Daniel and Jordan discuss advance preparations needed to make this experience enjoyable for Daniel's father. They mention Bubba's Shuttle Service multiple times. Daniel plans to contract Bubba to move people and equipment from Atkins, Virginia to the shelter on Saturday. I didn't realize I could catch a taxi in the wilderness. I lean toward Buddy and whisper, "Buddy, Bubba's Shuttle Service is a name to remember."

Buddy responds by reaching up and nuzzling my cheek with his cool, wet snout, then tucks in closer to my side. It's his way to say, *"I'll help you remember Bubba's name, Poppy."*

Buddy and I were chilly last night. We are freezing tonight. My sleeping bag liner and rain cover fail to keep me warm. I can't believe I dumped my sleeping bag on the trail last week. I left a cold weather bag behind in hot, humid weather; it was a good choice. Hiking without a sleeping bag in this temperature is foolish. When I shiver to warm my body, I rise from the floor, dig out my raincoat and rain pants from the backpack, and slip them over my clothes.

"Sorry guys," I whisper, when I see heads pop out from inside sleeping bags. Next time, I will rummage through my backpack with headlamp blazing before the people fall asleep.

I'm warm in no time. Buddy lies close, and before long, we are fast asleep.

The sun rises early. Everyone works together to clean the shelter and gets ready for a new day. Even Buddy is engaged. He works same as a panhandler on a street corner negotiating portions of our breakfast for himself.

Daniel and Jordan leave before I finish compressing equipment to fit in my pack. When Buddy returns from a walk in the woods, I place packs on our backs and head to work.

"It will be a good day, Buddy."

"Yes, it will, Poppy," I hear Buddy say through the jingle of his dog tags, as he moves past me to follow the scent left by Jordan and Daniel.

Chapter Fourteen
Wapiti Shelter

Buddy-Boy is frisky this morning. He serves as point man, delivering a strong pace as we descend Pearis Mountain's backside and climb to Sugar Run Mountain's ridgeline.

The foliage encasing our path is a magnificent array of greens, reds, oranges, yellows, and browns, mixed with brief splashes of crystal blue sky. The natural appeal of our habitat diffuses the physical punishment we accept to complete the 729-foot descent and the 1,184-foot ascent over 4.3-miles.

I'm glad Buddy halts when he comes to the wood sign marking the side trail to Woods Hole Hostel. Is my dog tracking Newt's and Kermit's scent this morning? The Georgia boys followed this side trail last night. Buddy may track friendly scent, but then again, he may stop to make sure I don't miss another important sign.

"Buddy, do you want to visit Woods Hole Hostel? We missed their hot breakfast. If we hurry, I'll bet you can join the yoga class. In fact, why don't you get a massage after yoga? Maybe the owner will comp your rubdown if I volunteer some time working in the hostel's garden."

Buddy's tail wags so hard his butt shakes as he walks the side trail to yoga class.

"Whoa Buddy. I'm sorry, pal. I'm playing with you. No yoga and massage this morning. Wapiti Shelter is today's destination."

Buddy's disappointed. His frown communicates a strong message: *"Poppy, lighten up on the schedule. When will we walk these woods, again?"*

My dog is right. Woods Hole Hostel has a great reputation. It's a shame I didn't make time to enjoy this wilderness treasure.

I didn't plan ahead, so Buddy and I move on in silence toward today's final-destination.

A few minutes later, a voice floats over the hilltop we work to reach. When we arrive at the hill crest, I can't attach a person to the voice. This is the first of many times we notice human sound without a person present: speech, singing, laughter, and play. Sounds piercing wilderness silence. I am startled for a moment and then remember sound travels distances when there's an absence of city noise.

Am I imagining a human presence? No, the voice has Buddy's attention. My dog walks beside me instead of behind me. Buddy-Boy is alert but not concerned. His tail wags behind the backside of his pack. He's focused straight ahead.

"Not to worry, Buddy-Boy. A man may stand around the next turn or he may be a mile away. It depends on wind and terrain conditions. Who knows, Phillip may be present, afloat without form," I half joke with my hiking companion.

I am not convinced the spirit of people who occupied this land before us do not walk with us today.

The voice takes form as the bending footpath straightens. A man talks on a white cell phone. As we draw close, he and I wave. When we pass on the path, we smile and nod to each other without speaking or stopping. The backpacker is engaged in an animated conversation with a person helping a child with algebra homework.

Buddy and I walk faster to give this man privacy. We stop to eat lunch when I find a cell connection for myself. I drop our equipment beside the footpath before I leave Buddy to try my call. My dog sprawls across the dirt trail to relax once I remove his pack.

"Buddy-Boy, let's eat when I get back. I have a hankering for smoked sausage, cheese, trail mix, and raisins with a Snickers bar for dessert." Buddy's eyes sparkle and his tail thumps the dirt when he hears the words 'eat', 'dessert' and 'Snickers bar'.

I call my friends in Roanoke to share Buddy's status. Adam and Maye are pleased to hear Buddy is back on his game. Adam addresses me as 'Santa Claus' and praises my holiday spirit when I whine, "I'm freezing at night."

"Jimmy Doug, this time of the year, fools hike elevation without a sleeping bag. Tell me again why you dropped your bag beside the trail last week? Oh, yes, I remember: you reduced equipment weight by two pounds."

I chuckle, then respond to Adam's playful mocking.

"For the record, I'm not complaining. I'm stating a fact. I froze last night until I added rain gear to my sleeping attire."

"Jimmy Doug, ignore this rude man," Maye chimes into the conversation. "Spot is working. Thank you very much for sending email updates through the GPS tracking device. I'm more comfortable accepting your crazy antics, since I can follow your progress on the computer."

We banter back and forth for a few minutes, then my friends sign off the call as Maye reminds me she and Buddy have a date Saturday afternoon. I'm grateful technology allows me to connect with caring people walking wilderness trails. Total isolation might become maddening after a time.

I see the voice rest on his knees and scratch Buddy's belly as I return to the clearing leading to my dog and equipment. The hiker waves when he notices me. The voice has a name. Ray is a man in his mid-forties. I do not catch his last name. He is athletic and fit, having survived the Appalachian Trail experience for several weeks. Ray took up residence at Woods Hole Hostel for a few days, working for room and board. He's re-joining the trail now.

Out of curiosity, I mention the trail name of the female who left the interesting journal entry I read at Niday Shelter. Ray smiles when I mention her trail name.

"She was a hostel guest when I arrived," he responds. "I understand she stumbled off the trail fighting food poisoning. She volunteered time to the hostel after Ms. Neville nursed her back to health. I enjoyed her company."

Ray's facial expression and tone of voice leave no doubt the message he intends to convey with his last statement. Ray is married with young daughters. He's a fellow Texan. I sense the emptiness he carries. Two lonely people connected at Woods Hole Hostel to satisfy short-term physical and emotional needs at the long-term expense of family and marriage. What will Ray carry home from the Appalachian Trail to share with his wife?

Ray continues his story while I cut into a sausage stick and a block of cheese I carry for lunch. Ray tells us his trail name is

R.I.P., short for 'Rest in Peace'. I call Ray by his birth name the entire time we are together.

I miss my family as I listen to Ray. A year has passed since we spent meaningful time together. My father and children still work to recover from the emotional train wreck Reece and I created for them when we tore our family asunder.

Ray just lost a powerhouse job working for a well-known corporation. Pain rests behind his eyes. They communicate more than his words. Ray received a solid severance package once he agreed to train the foreign workers who replaced his entire department. He walks the Appalachian Trail to regroup from this lifetime disappointment.

Ray is one of 3.2-million American citizens whose jobs U.S. corporations replaced with foreign workers between 2001 and 2013. These are millions of Americans. Employees who left home every morning and worked hard, many at the expense of personal relationships or long-term health. People who invested in their future. Breadwinners who married, had children, and are raising a family. Husbands and wives who paid taxes and made saving a priority for their children's education and their retirement. Americans who did their job and lost it to power they couldn't control by themselves.

I slow my pace while I struggle to understand a corporate culture that rewards undermining the American workforce by giving American jobs to foreign workers supporting foreign governments. How does America gain from this colossal display of greed? Wall Street profits while state and local government provides essential services for underemployed and unemployed workers. Has anyone observed price reductions offered at the cash register for goods and services they buy?

As I regain focus, I see my hiking partners move ahead, locked in private worlds. Both are oblivious to where I walk and what I contemplate. I sit on a rock outcrop to think and enjoy the freedom that comes facing open sky with feet dangling thousands of feet above the ground.

Buddy accepts Ray before I meet the man. My dog rolled on his back for a good belly-scratch when Ray tried to step over him on the trail. Ray started his journey at Harper's Ferry, West Virginia. His entry on the Appalachian Trail was a thoughtful plan.

He flew from Texas to Washington, D.C., took a train to Harper's Ferry, West Virginia, and toured the Appalachian Trail Conservancy before he set out on the trail. His commitments to family are to stay safe and finish at Springer Mountain, Georgia in time to share Thanksgiving at home.

I discover Ray and Buddy sitting on an outcrop that is overlooking the valley. Ray is reading from a religious self-help book, and Buddy is contemplating life, I guess. Based on the panoramic view, Ray selected a nice place to wait for my return.

"What do you know of Wapiti Shelter, Jimmy Doug?" Ray asks, after a long period of silence.

"Nothing important. I believe it's the next shelter on the trail. Why do you ask?"

"When I prepared for this trip, I read a *Washington Post* article describing a double murder that occurred in 1981 at the original Wapiti Shelter."

"Sweet Jesus," I express, as I flash back to questions I fielded from family and friends. They were interested in how I planned to protect myself walking alone on the Appalachian Trail. I told them I'd consider carrying a pistol in my pack.

My 357 Magnum will ease anyone's fears. If I hit where I believe I'm aiming, I can stop predators such as: bears, wild cats, hogs, snakes, and humans. I'm glad I own a menacing weapon. I rarely hit where I draw a bead. The revolver sits unloaded at home, high on a shelf. The weapon and ammunition weigh more than I'm willing carry in my backpack for personal protection on this trip.

Adam persuaded me to carry his long-knife under the pretense that the weapon served dual purposes: protection and a hole-digger. Backcountry etiquette dictates I cover poop when I drop a load on the ground. Adam wants me to use his expensive knife to cover my poop when no outhouse is in sight.

Buddy carried Adam's knife the first week. My logic was straight forward. If I needed the knife to defend us, I'd reach for Buddy, unzip his pack, and pull out the knife. We'd be dead before I secured the knife from my backpack. I left the knife with Adam when I picked up Spot in Roanoke.

The truth is: Simpson's Buddy-Boy is my defense. If Buddy-Boy can face a bear, I'm sure he can intimidate a man. If not, we will die fighting, together. That is how I romanticize my self-defense options, until I hear Ray's words. Now, I am forced to concede personal risk exists for well-intentioned backcountry travelers.

"A Pearisburg, Virginia man killed sleeping hikers in Wapiti Shelter. I can't remember whether the killer was staying with the couple at the shelter, or he stalked them while they slept. He shot the man in the head. He stabbed the girl with a long nail. She died fighting from the confines of her sleeping bag.

"What is most pathetic, Jimmy Doug is how the prison parole board released this double-murderer for good behavior after serving a 15-year sentence. Fifteen years for two precious lives. The killer returned to Pearisburg to live. A few years later, he attempted to murder two more people fishing and camping on the other side of Wapiti Shelter by Dismal Creek. We walk that trail section tomorrow," Ray says, concluding his story and returning us to forest silence.

"What happened to the killer?" I ask, after I've absorbed the horror behind his words. Ray answers the question as he points toward the valley running parallel to our path.

"He died in his prison cell for unexplained reasons. They buried him right over there, at a cemetery in Newport, Virginia."

Buddy steps to my side while Ray tells us his account of innocent life lost on this stretch of terrain. I reach for my Labrador when Ray finishes his story. I stroke my dog's head, then brush the length of his nose with my fingers. Buddy stops at my touch. I bend to his ear and whisper, "Not to worry, Buddy-Boy. We will be okay."

Buddy moves ahead and sets a new pace, serving as point man for our little squad of hikers. We spend the balance of the hiking afternoon listening to Ray explain his quest for religious understanding. I find his conversation interesting. Ray hasn't discovered what he believes. He shares what he's learned. I appreciate how Ray approaches his time with us. I understand this place in his life.

Ray and I walk the same trail today with a different purpose under Buddy's watchful care. I do not know Ray. When I listen to his words, Ray is here to discover a faith he can trust to free him from grief attached to his family's unexpected loss. When I regard his conduct, I discern that Ray has escaped to the Appalachian Trail to lick emotional wounds and medicate the pain of loss any way he chooses.

Security ripped from life is unsettling. The aftermath causes the actual damage. Ray lost a long-term career. I lost the life I struggled hard to build with Reece to share with our children and grandchildren through our retirement. I listen to Ray without offering comment. My thoughts are my own. If I confided in strangers, I'd share this with Ray:

"I've traveled your healing path. My pain compounded without relief and I created a new pain for innocent beings who offered me comfort's gift. I hope you find a different path to restoration in the quietness of these woods. Your family looks to you for leadership when you return home from the Appalachian Trail."

Wapiti Shelter sits in a valley surrounded by Sugar Run Mountain, Brushy Mountain, and Flat Top Mountain. Streams descend every mountainside to merge with Dismal Creek. Buddy leads us down Sugar Run's mountainside for 1,100-feet to reach the shelter around 4:00 pm.

Ray moves to the picnic table and drops his backpack. I stand at the edge of the camp site and take in what I see and absorb what my gut senses. I'm not comfortable. The building is new. The air is spoiled. A selfish man murdered innocent hikers engaged in a lifetime accomplishment in this vicinity. The couple walked the ground I walk. They finished tasks to end their hiking day I will finish for myself today. Friends drifted to sleep, expecting to wake up and share a new hiking day. I will close my eyes tonight and hope the same. Evil stole their lives and their families' dreams.

Since its early afternoon, I assume we'll find an empty shelter. But it's not empty. Fire burns in the fire-pit. Two sleeping bags lay open side by side on the shelter floor. Both bags are ruffled from use. Ray greets a talkative man in his late forties to early fifties wearing underwear and boots. A shy boy stands to the side. The quiet one is in his early twenties. He wears street clothes and street shoes. The boy does not appear to own hiking equipment.

Ray recognizes the shy one from the trail. The shelter inhabitants tell their stories. I do not believe the boy. I do not respect the man. Ray may be comfortable, but I'm uneasy in these surroundings. When we've lingered for a few minutes, I address Ray:

"Thanks for the nice day. It's still early, so we are leaving to make up for distance lost on Sunday. We'll sleep on the ground near Trent's Grocery. You are welcome to join us."

"You go ahead, Jimmy Doug. I'll pitch my tent over there and enjoy this fire tonight. I'll try to catch you before you reach the grocery store."

Every person is accountable for their own decisions. How we decide matters. Life paths alter for many people with just one decision. What will Ray bring home to share with his wife and daughters?

"We will see you on the trail, Ray. I hope you are right. I will buy the first hamburger."

Chapter Fifteen
Trent's Grocery

Uneasiness dissipates each step we take under Jefferson National Forest's tree cover. Since water saturates the ground, we walk on wood-plank foot bridges more than on the dirt.

Buddy is drawn to water whether it's okay to swim or not. My dog cannot wade in this swamp.

"Buddy, remember jumping into Catawba Creek our first morning on the trail? How heavy was your pack? Please stay on the footbridge."

Buddy-Boy is dry when a perfect campsite presents itself two miles from Wapiti Shelter.

"Buddy, let me check the map. If we are near Trent's Grocery, I say we spend the night. What do you say?"

Buddy lies by my side while I study my map.

"Five miles to VA606, then a brief walk to Trent's Grocery, Buddy-Boy. This campsite must be near the Dismal Creek campground. If we stay here tonight, we will sleep on ground the Wapiti Shelter Murderer stalked to murder more victims."

I laugh as Buddy nuzzles me. We walked away from one murder site to spend the night here.

"Buddy, do we stay or leave?" My dog rises and walks into Dismal Creek. He drinks from running water that swirls around his ankles, then casually makes his way into deeper water with his pack on his back. Buddy is playing with me. He stops before his pack touches the water.

Buddy decides. We sleep beside Dismal Creek tonight. He's right. Don't waste opportunities based on another person's disappointment. My experience is mine to earn.

"Buddy, take another step. You are welcome to swim in the cool night air. You carry your pack tomorrow, wet, or dry. Please understand, you're not sleeping next to me if you are wet."

Once we settle for the night, I email an update letting people know we're okay and we've stopped for the night. When I push the button, Spot signals a satellite. The satellite forwards the canned message to designated email accounts with specific GPS coordinates marking our location on a computer map.

Since I hike without a tent, I should seek protection from the elements. But not tonight. My head rests on the waterproof bag I carry my coat, rain gear, and clean clothes. My feet touch the backpacks I stacked beside my boots. Buddy settles beside me. My rain tarp covers everything. I stare through the open tree canopy and enjoy the last-of-day color mix with the first-of-night sky, waiting for the stars to arrive. I am home for the night.

The sound of moving water blending with insect songs lulls me toward sleep when I sense Buddy move. The next instant, I hear a large object crash through the woods. Buddy jumps up and sits at attention between me and the stream.

I believe a bear is foraging nearby.

Park rangers distribute reliable information when dangerous bears are present in hiking areas. I adhere to their warning protocol. Extreme protocol is not a priority for me in Central Virginia. Since I do not hang my food in a tree at night, I hope I've sealed everything a bear might find delicious.

I'm not sealed, so I open the big blade affixed to my Swiss Army Knife. The weapon is puny, but the knife is available to poke a bear if the furry creature gets serious. Poke once, maybe. Stab? Never. I'll cut my finger when the blade retracts on contact before I stab a bear while protecting Buddy.

I'm tempted to crawl beside Buddy and ask if he wants me to ring the bear bell. The outfitter in Alaska was adamant we needed the bell for bear protection. I wonder what advice he'd offer sitting beside me, now?

Believe it or not, Brad Pitt comes to mind at this distressing moment. Brad portrays a mountain man living with his father and brothers in Montana. Each brother loves the same woman. The movie ends for me with Brad fighting a Grizzly Bear with a knife resembling Adam's. The Grizzly Bear wins the fight. Brad marries Angelina, raises a family, sponsors humanitarian efforts, and lives other lives in other movies. I'll be bear-supper before I push Spot's 'Blackhawk-Down' button fighting a bear with a Swiss Army Knife.

Which direction does the wind blow? Fortunately, the breeze blows the bear's scent our way. Buddy and I stay still while I finish this mental checklist of useless thought. We stay quiet until wilderness hushes. I believe bear risk subsides, until I hear a tree trunk crack, break, and crash to the ground with a resounding thud. As these sounds merge and echo beyond our living space, we hear bear noise crash through underbrush in the opposite direction.

Buddy and I look at each other, then I exhale the long breath I've held awhile. The bear climbed a tree, rode it to the ground, then scurried home to tell the family.

Minutes pass before my heart rate returns to normal. Time evolves before I appreciate night sounds; even longer before I recognize the night sky is picturesque. Once I relax, I sleep under the watchful care of Simpson's Buddy-Boy. When I stir in the middle of the night, Buddy-Boy is sound asleep. If Buddy is asleep, bears in these woods must be asleep.

We wake with the sun shining bright. I expect Ray to stand over us any moment.

"Buddy, how did we oversleep?"

My dog is an astute observer of human behavior. Buddy lays his head on my chest and looks in my eyes with a confused expression.

"Poppy, hiking is exhausting. Did you set an alarm last night?"

Buddy-Boy and I skip breakfast and break camp. I apologize to my dog for disrupting the morning routine.

"Hang with me, Big-Guy. I promise I'll buy you a can of wet dog food when we reach Trent's Grocery."

Cheeseburger aroma flirts with my imagination until I see a bear cub cross our path and scurry into the woods. The bear resembles a pet, more than a predator. We stop to watch it play until I remember momma bear and other cubs must be in the vicinity.

I breathe deeply and exhale once we reach asphalt pavement. The morning trek is a challenge I didn't expect while sleeping on a valley floor. We hiked the Brushy Mountainside and still beat Ray to VA606. I am disappointed we had to rush this morning. We missed the chance to walk a short side trail to Dismal Creek Falls.

Buddy and I walk the gravel surface covering the roadside. Traffic moves fast in both directions. I consider Buddy my peer on the Appalachian Trail. He carries his weight and walks every step with me. Buddy may be a dog to the average person, but he is no longer a dog in my mind. He is my companion and backpacking partner.

I hope Buddy understands when I pull out his lead to attach to his collar. When I reach for him, my dog turns to accommodate me, then takes off for the trailhead at a dead run. He sprints toward an athlete riding a mountain bike in the middle of the road. The rider carries a sleeping bag in one hand and grips the handle bars with the other hand.

It's Adam. His dog races behind his bike. Ray is further back. Both men hustle toward us.

"Adam, what are you doing here? Aren't you working seven straight, 12-hour shifts at the hospital?"

"Jimmy Doug, you complained you freeze at night. Maye and I can't have 'Santa froze' listed as an accomplishment on our trail-boss resumes. Maye volunteered her credit card; I left work last night to buy you a sleeping bag at Wal-Mart."

"Thank you, Adam. It's great to see you. I'm surprised you found us in the forest."

"Spot told me where to search, Jimmy Doug."

"Smart. You read the GPS coordinates Spot provided with my last email."

"Yes, sir, Jimmy Doug. Do you remember the headlamp I bought when we shopped Gander Mountain? I planned to ride here last night using the big light. My wife stopped me before I changed my clothes."

"I believe you, Adam," I say with a smile on my face. Thank goodness for Karla. Adam has no fear. A wiser mind prevailed last night. "Adam, how was the bike ride?"

"Bike handling on this terrain with one hand was a challenge. I won't take this chance again, but I wanted to get you this sleeping bag."

Adam took risks providing this gift. It's against the law to ride a bike on the Appalachian Trail in the Jefferson National Forest.

Ray arrives wearing a big smile.

"Hello Jimmy Doug. Did you oversleep? I see you haven't arrived at Trent's Grocery."

"Damn Adam," I laugh to myself. *"We stop to talk, and Ray catches me before Buddy and I can get to Trent's Grocery."*

"First round of food and drink on me," I announce, before I introduce these men to each other.

This roadside is not the place to stand and chat with two active dogs playing by our sides. Yes, Buddy is now acting every bit the dog he can be, at this point. I give Adam money for our first hamburger orders and send him on his bike to Trent's Grocery.

The "Pearisburg Dance to the Outhouse" is a forgotten memory. I crave juicy cheeseburgers, greasy fries, candy bars loaded with sugar, real cokes, and ice cream for dessert. We sit on a park bench that leans against the grocery store front and devour three cheeseburger orders while laughing and telling stories. I keep my promise to Buddy. He swallows two cans of wet dog food.

I know Adam wants to walk this journey with Simpson's Buddy-Boy and me. He'd be an excellent thru-hiking partner. Adam's skilled, fit, carries his own load, and he steps up to offer aid before I realize I need help. What we want to do is conditional. What we do is live our responsibilities. Adam can't walk away to hike the Appalachian Trail. He's raising a family and building a career. When he leaves us, he promises to make time in his schedule to walk a section with me when I return to Roanoke and begin the trek north. It's good to keep dreams alive. I hope Adam keeps his promise, but I know he can't.

Chapter Sixteen
Central Kansas

Ray and I are alone tonight at Jenny Knob Shelter. Ray has built a nice fire for warmth and light. The quiet evening is relaxing. My boots and socks hang from a hook next to my backpack, and my hat on the shelter wall. I sip instant coffee mixed with hot chocolate and sweetener; a comfort drink I first enjoyed during my army days. I'm sure Ray can see I am lost in my thoughts, observing me through the fire's orange glow. I'm surprised when he speaks.

"Jimmy Doug, you and Buddy-Boy are kind and respectful. You listen and encourage. If you want to share, I'd appreciate listening to your story. What inspired you to take this journey?"

Buddy moves from the shelter floor and places his big head on my lap. I stay still for a time, watching flames change color and form. I don't share my story with anyone. Life is easier when I listen and mentor. It's painful to put words to my sadness.

I meet Ray's eyes across the fire pit and release my sorrow from the place I bury the hurt. Words form to articulate the pain stored in my memories, but I do not speak. I return to my thoughts and consider the words myself:

My mother's name is Letha Lee. Her end-of-life experience is the pivotal point that changes my life. When I arrived in Kansas, Mom was homeless. She was a patient at our hometown hospital. On a good day, she suffered from end stage renal disease. This day was not a good day.

My spirit lifted when I reached the city limits and recognized buildings lining familiar, brick paved streets. These Central Kansas streets, parks, playgrounds, schools, and homes helped create the best memories of my youth.

My ancestors migrated to this region from foreign lands in the 1800s. I visited their graves before I drove to the hospital. As I prepared to face my mother and share her dying days with her, I parked near the hospital's main entrance, and slid from my truck, wearing blue jeans and a starched, white dress shirt. I stepped onto the pavement for the first of countless times to come.

A hospitalist, named Sarah, introduced herself when I arrived at the third-floor nursing station. She was friendly and was a professional. Sarah escorted me to a private room where I met my mother's medical team. I sensed the medical center was braced for legal action. I drove 11-hours to support Mom and her medical team. Someone might have wanted to fight. But I didn't. I greeted each caregiver with a genuine smile and then sat back in my chair to listen to Sarah.

"Mr. Simpson, your mother had a vascular access problem related to her dialysis. A hospital in another town corrected the fistula malfunction. Your mother acquired a hospital-based infection during that admission. We admitted her to our hospital through the emergency room when her medical condition worsened. We have tried different procedures and medications with little success.

"Mr. Simpson, your mother's medical condition is grave. Your brother holds the medical power of attorney for your mother. He demands we stop treatment for the infection and take your mother off dialysis. Sam wants your mother placed on comfort care. Your brother threatens a lawsuit if we do not follow his instructions. You should be aware administration decided yesterday to have our security team escort your brother from the hospital. He is a potential risk to patients and staff. His behavior is irrational, and he acts threatening in front of your mother and other patients' families.

"Your mother is resting now. She is excited to see you. The nurses tell me she loves the flowers and card your family sent her," Sarah added, looking for a response.

"I am sorry Sam has placed everyone under this stress. No one deserves this added burden. He does not handle problems in a rational way. I understand the hospital's risk management strategy.

"Sarah, did you see Sam act out?"

"No," she responded, turning her eyes downward for the first time since we met. *"We work seven day shifts and my colleague was on duty."*

"What is your colleague's name?" I asked.

"Her name is Becca," Sarah responded. *"She'll meet you and answer any question you might have when she returns on Wednesday."*

"Was anybody in this meeting with my mother when my brother instructed the medical center to stop treating her?"

"I was," a soft spoken social worker responded.

"Can you tell me what happened?" I asked with a tone inviting the truth.

"Your brother stood over your mother and demanded the medical team let your mother die. Becca worked on the other side of your mother, taking out her PICC Line and removing her IV. Becca completed the last medical procedure just as your mother opened her eyes and spoke with clarity in her voice, asking Becca what she was doing. Mr. Simpson, everyone stepped back. No one knew your mother was conscious."

I leaned forward in my chair. My personal problems and concerns disappeared.

"What happened next?" I asked, with a tone I use when I don't want to hear the answer.

"Sam ignored your mother. He continued to berate Becca while she explained to your mother she was removing life sustaining care, based on her younger son's instructions. Becca asked your mother, 'Do you want to live, Mrs. Simpson?' Your mom responded with conviction: 'I want to live'. Your mother left no doubt for anyone in the room what she wished to do. It was clear to everyone but your brother. Your brother lost control. He shouted, 'No, she doesn't want to live. She doesn't understand what she is saying. Follow my instructions. Why are you ignoring me? I have the medical power of attorney. My mother doesn't remember her name. She doesn't know the year or where she is living. You are trying to make money off her. She is suffering. This needs to end now!'

"Mr. Simpson, we removed your brother to gain control over your mother's medical care," the social worker concluded, looking toward me for guidance.

I was stunned. I sensed the pain of betrayal my mother endured. Mom listened to my brother plead to end her life when she told the hospitalist she wanted to live. I did my best to hide my emotions, sitting with this medical team. I believed they too, bared raw emotions behind masks of professional etiquette.

This was surreal. My mind broke trying to grasp the emotional cruelty my mother endured at my brother's hand. Mom was a living human being. She had a name and a history. She was conscious and was fighting to live, yet Sam had legal say over Mom's life. He had the legal right to choose life or premature death for our mother. My brother saw my mother and heard her tell the hospitalist she wanted to live, and my brother demanded this medical team stand by and watch my mother die.

My mother has a former husband, two sons, five grandchildren and five great-grandchildren. No one in this legacy was protecting her, fighting for her, or walking with her to a peaceful end. My mother's advocates were the strangers sitting in this room with me at the time. These people deserved my respect and gratitude. They stood together against my brother for my mother's right to live. Now, they fought for her with their knowledge and skill to sustain her life. I rose from my chair and said as much. Then I asked:

"Can someone please direct me to my mother's room?"

Mom's room smelled clean. A large window funneled warm sunlight toward a hospital bed. The bed supported a speck of a body I did not recognize. The name plate affixed to the hospital room door reported the patient was my mother. This person was fragile as a helpless child, and she was alone. I did not sense death in her presence. I sensed life as I walked across the room. Once Mom opened her unmistakable eyes to greet me, I saw this patient was indeed my mother.

"Where have you been, Jimmy Doug?" Mom whispered through her smiling lips, cracked and missing their familiar red lip gloss. "I've waited for you to get here."

"Thank you for waiting, Mom. It took time to organize my life. You're my priority now."

She smiled, and her body relaxed.

"I am so glad you are here, son," she said, as she closed her eyes and returned to the dream world where she existed full-time.

A safe place where she retained an active heart beat in a dying body.

I watched her sleep for a few minutes, then moved around the room to find a hair brush, a washcloth, a dry towel, and lipstick.

"This is new territory for me," I laughed to myself.

I washed Mom's face, removed crust from her eyes, and stroked her skin with a soft towel. Mom's face was easy. Her hair was a challenge. I took the hair brush and released the tangles from her hair. When I'd tried my best, I applied lipstick to her lips. When I was done, I slid a reclining chair with a tall back next to Mom's bed, so I could wait for her time to end. When I was situated, Mom surprised me. She reached for my hand with her eyes closed and said to me, "Thank you, Jimmy Doug."

We held hands for hours. Mother dreamed. I considered how we both arrived here and what I could do to show her the love she had always deserved.

"Hi Son, you look nice," Mom said, as she squeezed my hand in the early evening. Her eyes sparkled with life.

"Thanks Mom," I replied. "Did you have a nice nap?"

Mom squeezed my hand, again, and returned to her world. She left me to view the busy traffic flowing outside her hospital room door. Much later, I saw Mom studying me.

"Are you with me, Mom?"

"I am, Jimmy Doug," she replied.

I was prepared to ask Mom the question I needed an answer to honor her wishes. How could I ask my mother if she was ready to die?

"Mom, have you considered your next life?"

"I have, son," she replied.

"Do you know where you are going?"

"Not yet," she replied.

"Mom, are you ready to find out?"

"No, Jimmy Doug. I've waited for you to get here."

"Okay, Mom," I said with a big smile. "Will you let me know when you are ready to leave?"

"I will, Son. But first, I want you to promise me you will take me to the old homestead."

That sentence is the longest Mom shares with me for several months.

"I'll take you to Geneseo. First, you fight hard to get well. Then, you must work hard to get your body ready. I will help you, Mom," I promised, committing myself to join her isolated world.

"I will try my best, son," she responded, as she went back to sleep with my promise secured in her heart.

After she ate, and the night shift came on duty, I placed the first of many goodnight kisses on my mother's forehead. The hospital was quiet when I left her room to find a place to eat and sleep in my hometown.

Floors gleamed when I entered the hospital lobby the next morning. The building bustled with busy people. I waved to the security guard manning his station at the main entrance and the gift shop attendant straightening stuffed animals in the window display. When I reached the elevator, I stopped to examine one of many original paintings hanging throughout this rich hospital.

When I stepped onto Mom's floor, I sensed positive energy emitted by people who enjoyed where they worked. As I turned the corner by the nursing station, I saw a small group of nurses congregating outside my mother's door. They were engaged in serious discussion with a hospitalist I had never seen. As I approached the group, one nurse looked my way and smiled. I could tell by her body language my mom was okay that morning.

"Hello, you must be Mrs. Simpson's son," the hospitalist extended a hand in a professional greeting. "My name is Becca. I will care for your mother the next seven days," she said, introducing herself.

Becca was a well-groomed professional, wearing a frumpy lab coat. She had stuffed her pockets with paper and small books. Her demeanor was impressive. She was an in-charge leader who exuded confidence and positive energy.

"So, you are the 'Other Sarah'," I responded with a kind smile. "I have been waiting to meet you. Thank you for everything you did to fight for my mom's right to live," I expressed with a tone of gratitude. "How is Mom this morning?"

"Your mother's progress is remarkable. Your presence is better than any medicine we can give." She must have noticed the sadness in my eyes because she added: "Your family is making a sacrifice with you so far away."

"The separation is challenging," I responded, and then added: *"I am heading home Friday. Will my absence be a problem for Mom?"*

"I don't know, Mr. Simpson. Your mother is getting stronger. She is happy you are here. Do you plan on returning soon?"

"I will come right back if she needs me," I replied. *"I will call her every day and I am hopeful the nurses will keep me updated on her prognosis. If you need me, I will come back,"* I added, as Mom's medical team looked at me without comment.

"We will keep you informed, Mr. Simpson," the hospitalist promised with a professional tone.

I expressed my sincere gratitude, again, as I shook hands with Becca and moved toward my mother's room.

"Don't be concerned, Mr. Simpson. We sent your mother to the dialysis room. Her treatment lasts three to four hours. You are welcome to stay in her room."

The medical team moved to the next patient's room, and I headed to the nurses' station to get a fresh cup of coffee. I stopped when I noticed the social worker sitting at her station. I hoped she could direct me to the Legal Aid Office.

Mom could not afford an attorney. My brother had turned Mom into an indigent. He stole her assets, then applied for Medicaid on her behalf. I was impressed with my brother's capabilities to carry out this level of theft.

Mom was a wealthy woman. Sam cleaned her out before he brought Mom to Kansas to die. My brother sold her home and other assets with the power of attorney my mother signed for him. Then, he cleared out her bank accounts, including the one where Mom deposited her social security checks. Mom did not have a dime to her name.

The social worker gave me the Legal Aid phone number. I called, and the attorney scheduled an appointment to visit Mom. Since I had time, I toured the hospital before I returned to Mom's room to wait. I enjoyed walking the halls and greeting patients, family members, and staff. A smile and kind words were easy to give.

I brought Bill Bryson's book, A Walk in the Woods to keep me company that week. That book was an entertaining story in-

volving two normal guys trying their hand walking the Appalachian Trail. If I couldn't prepare for my hike, I would live the journey through someone else.

Mom improved each day. We enjoyed simple fun together. The lively debates over politics and sports were no longer present. We limited verbal conversations to straightforward questions and easy answers when Mom was awake and aware. Real communication took place through a single touch or eye contact.

Our joy came from being together. I appreciated the opportunity to listen to my mother breathe and watch her sleep. It was a privilege to feed her, cheer her on with each bite she swallowed from a tray of food she could not consume. It was an honor to fetch her ice and prepare her drinks, knowing she would not drink a drop without my help.

I appreciated the time caregivers spent educating me on how Mom gained from the medication she received. Her blood pressure was dropping to an acceptable level and her infection was coming under control with the cocktail of antibiotics she was receiving by IV.

I was not comfortable leaving my mother, but my life was in Austin. If I went home, I could lay a foundation that could get everyone involved with mother's transition. I was still hopeful my wife would come to Kansas with me or support me transporting Mom back to a nursing home in Austin, Texas. The start would be awkward for sure, but we had handled more difficult challenges in our life together.

I wished my family was here with Mom. Living another person's reality changes perspective, creates understanding, and facilitates genuine forgiveness.

Friday was my fifth day in Kansas. When I arrived at the hospital that morning, the local radio predicted a snow storm would arrive early that afternoon. Winter comes fast in Kansas. I ran the town's circumference Sunday afternoon in shorts and a singlet.

I wanted to go home for a brief visit. It was worth a 22-hour-round-trip drive to be with my wife and children. If I left by noon, I would miss the flurries. If I drove straight through, I would be home to see my wife that night by 11:00 pm.

My wife and I worked well together to set aside disagreements to resolve problems. When we solved our predicaments, contentions were no longer a schism. I was hopeful my wife recognized the change in my countenance and would want to share this experience with me.

Snow was a minor inconvenience that morning. Leaving Mom was my concern. How could I tell her I was going home? She was fighting hard and her prospects for living improved every day I stayed with her.

Mom was in the Dialysis Treatment Room when I arrived on her floor. Since I would leave later that morning, I took a chance and walked straight into the room with the machines. Mom was one of two patients receiving treatment.

Mom was in good spirits. She appreciated the equipment and loved the people who cared for her three days a week, every week for the time she lived.

I held Mom's hand and listened while the technician shared her personal story. When I looked at my mother, she had closed her eyes. She was at peace in her world. I let her rest without interruption as the machine filtered her blood and monitored her vital signs.

The treatment room filled with new life and positive energy when Becca entered to make rounds. She was ready for 'Frontier Day', dressed in a lab coat, western shirt, jeans, and cowboy boots.

"Wake up, Mom. You will want to see this. Your hospitalist is a real Texas-Cowgirl," I chuckled, as Becca approached us.

Becca was amused by my response to her wardrobe choice. "We have a tradition we enjoy one weekend each year honoring our frontier heritage, Mr. Simpson. Besides, it's fun dressing same as you Texas cowboys from time to time. How is your Mom today?" she asked, then placed her stethoscope in her ears and leaned over to check my mother's upper body before I could respond.

When she finished her examination, Becca clasped the ear piece around her neck and allowed the stethoscope to fall against the front of her flannel shirt. Becca moved closer to Mom and gently brushed the hair from Mom's forehead before she asked my mother to open her eyes.

Mom smiled when she saw Becca.

"Good morning, Mrs. Simpson. I see you have your son with you. How are you today?"

Mom looked at me then stared at the hospitalist. My mother expected me to answer for her.

"She is good this morning. Aren't you, Mom?" I responded, without knowing how my mother felt.

Mom looked at me with loving eyes and answered, "Yes."

"I am happy for you, Mrs. Simpson. You have worked hard this week to get better. I know your son is proud of you. I am proud of you."

"Yes," Mom said again. She nodded her head this time. Mom was pleased with herself and so was I. She was still a fighter.

When Becca finished checking Mom's IV and dialysis access point, she addressed me while she held Mother's hand.

"So, Mr. Simpson, your mother is stabilizing. Lee should be ready to go back to her friends at the nursing home in another week to two weeks. I'd suggest you make plans to go home and be with your family. Make plans together. Your mother is strong. She will wait for your return. Won't you Lee?" Becca asked my mother.

Mom closed her eyes and turned her head away from the hospitalist.

"Mom, I know you are awake. Please listen. I need to visit our family to make sure they will be okay while I stay with you. I promise you I will come back for you."

"When?" my mother asked me.

"Soon," I answered, as my mother's son, my father's son, my wife's husband, my children's father, my grandchildren's poppy, and my clients CPA. I hurt as I watched disappointment move across Mom's face. The healing energy left the room. "I will come back, Mom. You will see. We have a trip planned to visit the Old Homestead."

Mom rested in her room after the treatment. I stood in front of our window and listened to her breathe. Snowflakes were accumulating on the ground.

"You need to go home now, Jimmy Doug," Mom said.

I watched snow fall to hide my tears from Mom.

"I know. It is snowing, and I need to sign paperwork at the nursing home before I drive to Texas."

"Go, Son. I'll be here when you return. Kiss my babies for me," Mom said in a strong voice.

"Get stronger, Mom. We have a trip planned to Geneseo," I said, as I placed a light kiss on her lips and walked out of the room.

"I will, Sonny-Boy," Mom replied, as I turned around at the door to wave goodbye.

My walk with Mom started in October 2012. It was now March 2013. In between these dates, we celebrated Halloween, Thanksgiving, Christmas, New Year, and Valentines with our nursing home family. We endured an icy, blustery Kansas winter commuting from the small town where her nursing home existed, and the next biggest town where the dialysis center resided. Mom fought through medical issues with the help of dialysis staff, emergency room staff, and critical care staff at the hospital. Sometimes, poor nursing care management at the nursing home caused her medical issues. Each time my mother failed, she rallied. Mom kept her word. She worked hard to get strong, and we made our trip to the old homestead in Geneseo, Kansas.

I stood by the nurses' station at the dialysis center. The charge nurse was explaining their new medical record software implementation plan when Mom's machine sounded a warning alarm. The equipment showed Mom's blood pressure was dangerously high. Mom sat patiently. Her countenance was calming for me. She was at peace with me and the people she considered her friends. The nurses did their job—work that had provided successful outcomes for us in the past. But not on that day.

"Mom, the nurses called an ambulance for you. We are making another trip to the hospital."

Ambulances transported Mom to the hospital regularly. That day was different. I could see it in Mom's eyes and in the nurses' demeanor. When my mother left the dialysis center, she would never return to her friends to receive life-sustaining treatment.

"I don't want to go to the hospital, Jimmy Doug. I want you to take me home with you to see my babies."

"Mom, I'd be happy to take you home. How will we get to Austin? Remember the last time I tried to lift you in and out of the truck?"

"I want to go home, Son."

"Mom, I understand. I wish we didn't have to go to the hospital, but we do," I gently said.

The nurses stepped back to allow the ambulance team space to prepare my mother for her last trip to the hospital. I could not believe this scene was unfolding in front of my eyes.

Rural hospitals face challenges recruiting top-flight-physicians to live in small towns. This hospital maintained quality patient care, back-filling staffing requirements with foreign physicians and locum tenum physicians.

Mom and I met a new locum physician in the emergency room's draped confines. The physician treated Mom as a new patient, ordering an extensive group of tests to meet hospital protocol. Tests Mom had suffered through many times. Results and treatment plans documented multiple times in Mom's electronic medical record by bright physicians and physician assistants at this hospital. Caregivers had worked together with Mom to keep her alive for months. New tests would not deliver a cure. My mother was dying.

"Mom, are you ready for more tests?"

"No, Jimmy Doug."

"I'm sorry, Doctor. My mother does not consent to another round of tests."

"I'm sorry, Mrs. Simpson. I can't admit you to a hospital floor without formal documentation. We need test results."

"Doctor, if you will look at her medical record, you will see the information you need for admission and treatment. The hospital admits Mom to the Critical Care Unit when she presents with these symptoms. I appreciate your need to follow protocols for admission and thank you for your courtesy and understanding, tonight."

The physician listened intently while he evaluated Mom. When he finished his physical examination, he smiled, patted me on the back, gently touched Mom's leg and told us:

"I'll be right back."

He stepped through the curtain wall 15 minutes later. He smiled at Mom, then said:

"Mr. Simpson, the Senior Hospitalist is on duty tonight. I understand you are friends. He is admitting your mother to the Critical Care Unit. Transportation is coming to take her to her room. God be with you, Mrs. Simpson."

Mom slept for days. My aunt and I sat with her. We watched excellent caregivers deliver their best to fight Mom's infection and rising blood pressure. She did not rally.

My mother's medical condition was grave. We started our walk to new life when Mom's medical condition was grave. Six precious months later, I faced the same decision my brother made on my mother's behalf. My aunt, the nephrologist team members, and the hospitalist team members offered sound counsel. Each caregiver made sure I understood the decision to place my mother on comfort care was my choice. I took their words home that night, knowing Mom and I were both loved by strangers.

The next morning, Mom was alert and in good spirits when she returned from her dialysis treatment. I was glad my aunt was present to share this time with us.

"Mom, you are the best partner I've worked with in my career."

Mom smiled, and her eyes sparkled. She knew I meant what I said.

"Remember when you ran our company? Can we talk this morning same as the old days?"

Mom didn't speak, but she looked at me with pride and affection.

My aunt moved to the bed and sat with her sister while I stayed in my chair next to her bed.

"Mom, have the angels told you where you are going when you leave this life?"

Mom smiled and nodded a 'yes'.

"Are you ready to move toward your new life? Grandpa, Grandma, and Sonny are waiting for you. They've waited a long time to hold you in their arms. Your mom and dad and brother are ready to embrace you and share the love they have stored for you."

Mom's response was: she closed her eyes. My aunt and I shared a smile through tears. I leaned over the bedrail and gave my mother a kiss on her nose.

"Mom, you are awake. I need your help. Please answer my question."

Mom took her time. When she opened her eyes, she shared a knowing smile with her sister.

"Son, do you need an answer right this minute?"

With those words spoken, an overwhelming sense of love filled the room. Sisters and son laughed together. Mom was walking to new life.

Becca offered her furnished basement to Mom, so she could spend her last days with me. The Hospice Team was waiting when I drove up with Mom in my truck. We worked together to help Mom get settled. The social worker and nurse explained administrative procedures, options for extended help with bathing, and instructions for administering pain medication. Another group of caring and capable professionals supported Mom and me.

When Becca's home cleared, Buddy and I headed to the basement to stay with Mom. Buddy-Boy made a place for himself next to me on the floor beside Mom's bed. Except for brief food and bathroom breaks, Buddy stayed by Mom's side until she passed away.

Mom stayed with me and her sister for seven days. I struggled to stay awake during her last night but couldn't. When I woke up with the sun, I laid on the couch beside Mom's bed. She was awake, memorizing my face while she touched the top of Buddy's head.

"Good morning, Mom."

"Good morning, Son."

"Mom, how does a hot cup of black coffee sound to you?"

"Yummy," was her response.

Mom was alert when I returned with two steaming cups. She took her time to enjoy the aroma she loved. Mom sipped a small taste of hot drink before she closed her eyes for good. She was content and secure in her surroundings.

My aunt arrived within the hour. We sat in silence. Mom's body was living out its final hours. I tried my best to support Mom's pain medication needs. I was grateful Becca was with us. She lent her ability when we asked.

Becca's basement had filled with new spiritual energies: pure peace, joy, and love.

When afternoon turned to early evening, I sensed Mom's spirit lift from her body. Her soul lingered with us before she mixed in with the new spiritual energy surrounding us. Mom was present—encouraging me while her body struggled for a time to stop breathing. When Mom's body took its last breath on its own terms, my aunt looked at me.

"I think Lee's gone, Jimmy Doug. Please ask Becca to check if my sister has passed away."

I smiled through soft tears. My aunt has always been present for me. She helped raise me when I was a boy being a boy, and a boy trying to be a young man. For these many months, she has stood by me, holding me close and helping me be a good man and a good son.

"Mom's gone now. Her spirit left a few minutes before her body stopped breathing."

When Mom passed, I stood by Buddy without purpose. The life I lived for 33 years closed. No mulligan was granted. Emotions I held back in Kansas were released, and I fell with no one to catch me. I turned to the Appalachian Trail to restore my confidence and start life anew.

When I finish reliving this memory, I answer Ray's question.

"Ray, my story is inconsequential. Buddy and I walk this trail to discover a new life. Today has been a good day. Let's enjoy the fire."

Chapter Seventeen
Big Walker Motel

Jenny Knob had three fixed walls with an open front when I closed my eyes last night. Rain cascades from the roof edge to form a fourth-wall this morning. Why should I get dressed to step into a downpour? Since I don't punch a time clock, it's easy to convince myself to stay in my sleeping bag, where I'm warm and dry. I glance across the shelter to check Ray's status. He's awake but isn't making a move to start his day.

"Any idea when it will stop raining, Ray?"

"I don't know, Jimmy Doug. I can't access the weather channel," he chuckles.

"What should we do, Buddy? Do we stay dry or get ready to hike in this downpour?"

"Let's get wet, Poppy," Buddy responds, pushing his nose against my side.

"Okay, wet feet today, Sweet-Boy," I say aloud, as I unzip the sleeping bag and rise from the floor. "If you want to hike this morning, then we hike. I carry pairs of dry socks in my pack, and I restocked on superglue and band aids when I was in Roanoke."

Buddy's confused by my last statement. I haven't suffered with blisters since I superglued the first batch and bought new boots and socks. The answer is simple: immersion foot is a nuisance I developed walking wetlands in the Army. Forty years later, my feet still get cold and numb when I'm forced to wear wet boots and socks for extended periods. Worse: the skin that rejects blisters embraces them as a new best friend.

I purchased expensive waterproof boots at Gander Mountain to reduce risk of immersion foot. What did I receive for the extra money I spent on upgraded boots? The boot name includes the word "waterproof". Waterproof is not a distinguishing characteristic of Keen Waterproof Boots in these conditions. In fairness to Keen, I'm not sure companies make light-weight hiking boots to withstand water in the conditions we face today.

Footwear is a popular conversation topic between thru-hikers. My informal polling suggests every hiker's waterproof shoes soak water same as a sponge and hold moisture long after we finish sloshing through the drainage ditch known as the 'Appalachian Trail'. Most seasoned hikers reject waterproof shoes early in their journey. My opinion: spend money on lightweight, quick-dry footwear you trust.

I dress for rain and pack carefully. I secure the equipment and food in waterproof bags. When my backpack is ready, I seal it with a waterproof liner, then pull the drawstring tight. Buddy doesn't have this luxury. His pack will get drenched. I hope the dog food I place in my pack will compensate for the extra water weight he will tote today.

Buddy and I stand together with packs on our backs and wait for Ray. I focus on the water wall we must penetrate to begin the work day. After several days walking this challenging trail, I'm surprised I'm intimidated by heavy rain. I wear expensive rain gear to protect my equipment and my body. If anyone should complain, it's Buddy-Boy. He doesn't own rain gear.

"Not to worry, Sweet-Boy. Let's adapt and have fun," I say, committing the day to action when Ray steps through the water curtain. "Buddy, let's be cautious hiking Brushy Mountain's ridgeline. Footing will be treacherous climbing 3,500-feet and dropping 3,600-feet in the pouring rain."

Simpson's Buddy-Boy leads. I follow as he steps off dry flooring into the deluge. My rain gear works as promised, with one important exception: my waterproof coat has an open collar. The jacket is stylish, hanging on an outfitter's clothes rack. Unfortunately, fashion statements don't obstruct runoff in a straight downpour. Rain trickles through the opening, along my back, to my backside.

"Note to self, Buddy-Boy," I laugh. "Next time I buy a $200 rain jacket, I will insist it has a hood."

My dog stays wet, hiking in direct rainfall and residual moisture percolating through thick tree cover. Since I perspire profusely wearing protective covering in warm weather, I'm not sure I receive any advantage wearing my jacket, today. Once water pours over the boot tops and soaks my socks, I change my mind-set from frustration to amusement. Last week, we suffered drought conditions. I happily accept wet clothes and boots today.

Ray is a 'news hog'. Trail journal entries are Ray's wilderness newspaper. Hikers leave hand written messages in spiral notebooks at shelters. Their comments remind me of grocery store tabloid articles. I never know what to believe. Ray is a devoted fan. He stops at each shelter to scour the local news source for information on current trail conditions, bear alerts, and hiker gossip.

We travel eight miles before we climb today's highest ascent, then dig heels and poles into the soggy footpath to descend a slippery slope. Once we reach flatter ground, Ray leads us on a side path to Helvey's Mill Shelter. Ray reads, and I explore. I'm impressed someone has displayed matchbooks at the shelter advertising 'Big Walker Motel' and 'Bubba's Shuttle'. I'd enjoy meeting the person with gumption to walk these woods to distribute marketing take-aways to thru-hikers. Maybe we should stay at the Big Walker Motel tonight.

"Buddy, do you want to stay at a motel tonight? We can dry clothes and equipment, get warm in a hot shower, and sleep on a real bed."

Buddy's never stayed at a motel. He's indifferent to the amenities Big Walker Motel offers tonight. He perks up when I speak the words, 'wet dog food'. Buddy-Boy doesn't waste time rising from his resting position. He places my hiking poles in his mouth, walks across the shelter floor, and drops the equipment at my feet. Big Walker Motel is now our destination.

We start the descent toward Bland, Virginia, and Big Walker Motel when we leave the Helvey's Mill Shelter side trail. The downhill walk is difficult in these conditions. Each step matters. The terrain is demanding, but not extreme; descending 720-feet the last 1.3-miles to VA612. The challenge this afternoon is staying on our feet. We wear soaked boots, walk steep downgrade, and negotiate sharp bends on slick ground.

A large boulder blocks my progress when I finish a complicated drop around a hard turn a half-mile from the paved road. The rock blocks an abrupt plunge to a steep ravine. I halt beside this way-station, because the passageway ends. The Appalachian Trail footpath rests on a ledge 15-yards below my boots.

I don't know why the pathway ends at the boulder. Maybe we missed a trail marker. The weather may have washed out the trail. Either way, we need to bridge this gap to reach the trail. Buddy joins me to assess our predicament. A four-foot flat surface named 'Appalachian Trail' separates the slippery terrain where we stand and the ravine's bottom. Add snow, and I stare at a 'black diamond' ski run without moguls.

My options are straightforward: I can retrace steps to re-engage the Appalachian Trail's surface. Retreat isn't my only choice. I can descend here. The question is: can I stop my descent on the Appalachian Trail before I slide to the ravine bottom?

I remember trying to teach Lacey to ski in Durango, Colorado. She skied the rope tow with confidence. She balked when time came to ski the bunny run. My little girl used her bottom, hands, and boots to "ski" to the bottom. The safest way to handle this grade is mimic Lacey: rest against my backpack and ride my butt until my feet meet the footpath. I can live with a bruised bottom. The next best solution is stay on my feet and traverse the slope the way I ski moguls on a snow-covered mountain, one sharp hop-and-turn at a time.

"What's the plan, Buddy?" I say aloud, staring at the ravine.

Buddy rests on his haunches and shifts his eyes between me and the ravine. Buddy says, *"Go for it, Poppy. I'm right behind you."*

"What do you think, Ray? Any suggestions?"

"No, I will lean against this boulder and watch you, Jimmy Doug. Be careful. If you make it to the trail unscathed, I'll follow the path you blaze."

"Okay. Here it goes."

I stand sideways to the ravine and hop off the trail side. *Why did I jump?* I question myself in mid-air. I plan to use my boots as dirt skis; digging edges into the grade, hoping they act as snow skis sliding on edge parallel to a slope.

The moment my boots land on the wet surface, I ride downhill on my side. Fortunately, my feet jam against the Appalachian Trail and I stop. I'm muddy, safe, and lying on solid ground. Ray laughs hard while Buddy leans over the edge and shakes his head. I smile as I stand and scrape mud.

"Come on, Big-Boy. It's your turn."

Buddy drops his butt, plants his forelegs and power slides to the trail. His advance is mature and fun to watch. Ray's good humor ends with his first step. One simple foot movement executed without thought. His boot slips on the slippery soil and Rays falls hard. His chest slams against the boulder. The obstacle stops my companion's momentum and prevents a serious accident. Ray is in a precarious position.

I move to station myself below the boulder to stop him if he falls. Buddy senses my thoughts and moves beside me. Before I can climb to Ray, he releases his hold, falls hard, and slides on his belly to the path. We stop him once he reaches the footpath.

Ray is either bruised or has broken his ribs. I'm not sure it matters. Either way, he struggles to breathe. The weight from his backpack isn't helping his pain. I unbuckle the straps and gently remove his equipment.

Buddy moves near Ray and provides comfort while I open my first aid kit to secure several ibuprofens, then grab a water bottle from Ray's pack. Ray ingests the only pain medication we carry.

We sit together in silence for a long time. I consider ways to help Ray off this mountain as he fights his pain and pushes away the thought he's finished walking the Appalachian Trail.

"Ray, I can call for help with Spot if phone coverage isn't available."

"No, Jimmy Doug. I'm walking to the trailhead. I'll call for a ride into Bland when we reach the road."

"You know best, Ray. Let me help you with your equipment," I say, as I reorganize both our packs and take what I can carry. Ray still totes most of his equipment and supplies. He finishes the mountain descent in pain without complaint.

Once we reach the trailhead at VA612, I pull out the matchbook I grabbed at the shelter and call the motel. I book two rooms, learn the town has medical providers, and ask if the motel will contact Bubba to pick us up at the location I describe. It turns out, Bubba is standing next to the woman I converse with on the phone.

Bubba arrives within 15-minutes. He is helpful, and I appreciate his calm temperament. Bubba manages Ray's equipment, then he gently maneuvers Ray into the cab of his late model Ford truck.

Buddy and I jump into the pickup bed. My dog finds space and lies on the floor. I sit on a spare tire and rest against the cab's back wall. I smile as a rough day's tension is released. Much has changed since Buddy and I crawled into the back of Mark's pickup to begin day three. Thanks to Mark's leg up, we are proving to each other we can survive on the Appalachian Trail.

When Bubba reaches town, he stops at a convenience store for Ray, then drives us to the Big Walker Motel. Bubba is a nice man and his rate is fair. When we check into our rooms, Bubba and his wife offer Ray a ride to the Bland Family Clinic and offer to drop me at the general store.

Ray declines the gift. He heads to his room to shower, self-medicate, and sleep. Buddy and I go to Dollar General to buy canned dog food and high calorie snacks we both enjoy. The grocery store shelves are stocked with gross food I never eat at home. I pile it into my hand basket today. Honey buns, cheese, sausage, chips and salsa, and chocolate milk top my shopping list.

Ray is a stubborn man. We sit outside my room and watch the evening sky draw its curtain across the Jefferson National Forest. Ray sips beer while we share the large pizza I ordered.

"What's your plan, Ray? Bubba will drive you to an Urgent Care Center."

"I know, Jimmy Doug. No reason to incur the expense. I'm fine. I plan to leave with you in the morning."

Ray believes he will head out with me in the morning. This man suffered pain masked in fear's adrenaline to reach the roadside this afternoon. I'm not sure how he plans to lift—let alone, carry a full pack tomorrow. I hope Ray is right. He values his time on the Appalachian Trail. If he can carry his backpack, I am confident Ray will finish his journey in the time his family has provided.

Buddy and I both take showers tonight. I turn the thermostat to high heat before I slip into my bed. If I'm lucky, the warm air will dry my waterproof boots. If my boots are free from moisture, the clothes I washed in the sink will dry.

Buddy stretches out next to me on the floor. I call my daughter and I write my grandson a letter. Buddy lies on his side and watches. When I turn off the lamp, I make sure Buddy is comfortable and sleeping. He's not. He's lying in the same position with the same expression on his face.

"Okay, Buddy-Boy, I get it. We walk the same steps. Come here. If I sleep on a bed, you should sleep here, too."

Buddy jumps up and takes his half from the middle of the bed before I can stake my claim to reasonable sleeping quarters. Once my dog is comfortable, he slides his hulking body right next to me, moving me closer to the bed's edge.

"Sweet dreams, Buddy," I say, kicking myself for spreading clothes and equipment across the room's second bed.

We rise with the sun. I slip on my damp clothes and wet boots and walk to the motel office seeking free coffee. I share a cup with Bubba as he discusses the weather, and we agree to a time he will carry us back to the trailhead.

Ray stands at my door when I return to my room. This Texan suffers this morning. If I had a say, I'd tell Bubba to drive Ray to Roanoke's airport to fly home. I don't have a say, so I offer a compassionate smile.

"Jimmy Doug, you're on your own. I hired Bubba to drive me to Troutdale, Virginia tomorrow for sixty-dollars. The Troutdale Church Hostel accepts donations. I'll volunteer labor to the church and share time with the pastor until I heal."

I smile and listen without comment. This is Ray's plan. When he's through laying out his idea, I share my breakfast with him before I leave to meet Bubba. We consume: cold pizza, honey buns, chips, and warm chocolate milk.

When I shut the motel room door, I give Ray my phone number, and ask him to keep me posted on his status. I don't hear from Ray, again. I never knew his last name.

Chapter Eighteen
O'Lystery Pavilion

Bubba adds motor oil to his Ford's engine, tosses the can in the pickup bed, then drops the hood when he sees us walking from our room toward him.

"Good morning, boys. Where you headed this morning?" he asks, as he wipes engine filth from his hands with a red cloth.

"Please take us to the IH77 overpass near US52, sir."

"No problem, Jimmy Doug. Toss your packs in back. Hey Buddy-Boy, come sit by me. I need help to navigate this morning."

My dog's rear end shakes with excitement as he hops into the vehicle and plops his bottom on the bench seat next to our chauffer. Bubba works the floor-mounted stick shift until the truck reaches highway speed and then shouts my name over wind and engine noise.

"Hey Jimmy Doug, I checked the weather forecast for you. Expect high wind and hard rain on the mountain tomorrow night."

Buddy glances my way. We both remember the hardship we endured trekking Sinking Creek Mountain ridgeline to Sarver Hollow Shelter in our first mountain storm.

"Thanks, Bubba. I appreciate you checking the forecast for us. We'll cut Friday's hike short and stay at Knot Maul Branch Shelter."

Fifteen minutes later, we stand alone on the Appalachian Trail with backpacks intact and hiking poles in my hands. Simpson's Buddy-Boy and I walk 19 miles the next two days. We track Brushy Mountain and Garden Mountain ridgelines to Chestnut Knob Shelter, then hike Chestnut Ridge to ascend and descend Lynn Camp's mountainsides before we cross over Lynn Camp Creek and return to Brushy Mountain.

The sky is blue, and the wind is calm when I remove our packs this afternoon. Knot Maul Shelter is empty. We relax with birds, crawling and flying insects, and scampering squirrels who chase each other across the ground to climb and leap from tree to tree.

Two southbound female thru-hikers approached us on a footbridge today. I enjoyed seeing lively faces and hearing kind voices. The women waved hello, shared a few pleasantries, patted Buddy on the head, and scratched the sweet spot on his back. Once their earphones were back in place, they raced past us, as if they were late for an important meeting. No more human contact today.

I sit on the picnic table spending time with my grandchildren. Hikers are known to keep a trail journal. I prefer writing letters. These one-sided conversations are my way to include my grandchildren on this journey. Sunlight filters through the tree canopy as I place a pen to the writing tablet. The wind blows leaves that will soon separate from their branches and return to the earth. Nature's music soothes my spirit when I take time to listen.

As soon as I finish my grandson's letter, I step around the shelter to make sure Buddy stays away from trouble. He is chasing squirrels. Buddy-Boy focuses on his job when we walk trails. He never leaves my side to chase a forest resident. When we relax, he loves to explore and play.

We are asleep before the sun sets. Bubba's prediction is right. Wind blows hard throughout the night, but it does not rain. This is my first contact with strong winds on a mountainside. Gusts whistle through the forest and slam against the shelter's side wall. The sound makes me anxious. The first blast is frightening when it rattles the shelter. I am thankful we are secure in a building protected by trees capable of withstanding this force. I will face this wind again, sleeping on open ground at Apple Orchard Mountain's summit. That struggle will be less pleasant.

Buddy and I wake at dawn to a dog pack barking in the far distance. The sound is a new noise. Buddy is agitated. I watch him pace the camp ground, then re-trace yesterday's steps on the trail for brief stretches. He hardly touches his breakfast.

I hope the wilderness is playing tricks with the sound, again. These howls, bays, and barks may come from a group of hounds chasing deer for a poacher several miles away. The way Buddy behaves, I am concerned we face a fast-moving pack of wild dogs. I'm uneasy sitting on the picnic table drinking coffee and eating oatmeal and pop tarts. I throw my coffee on the ground and work fast to finish morning chores.

It's not raining, but it will. I place the rain cover over my backpack and pull it tight. I'm not wearing rain gear this morning. The temperature is comfortable. Sweat soaked my clothes when we walked to Bland, Virginia. Rain can soak me today. We secure our packs to our backs as the dogs bellowing cries reach the long ascent to our shelter. It is time to leave the Knot Maul Branch Shelter.

I'm not sure why movie trivia sticks with me, but I'm glad it does this morning. Burglars always distract vicious guard dogs with food. Feed a dog if you want to stop a dog. I unzip Buddy's pack and remove the food he carries. We trot downhill toward the bawling noise and scatter several days of Buddy's food in a concentrated circle. I'm betting the distraction will delay the pack long enough to create distance between them and us.

We scale rough terrain for 0.9-miles before we start the descent. I won't tell you Buddy and I ran the first mile this morning. I will tell you we traveled our fastest pace to date. Brushy Mountain is silent when we slow to catch our breath before we begin the descent.

"Buddy, sounds as if we ruined the poachers' hunt when the dogs stopped to eat your food."

Buddy shakes his head as the sky opens and pours water.

"Poppy, food may have slowed the pack, but nature stopped the dogs this morning."

Severe storms give notice. The sky darkens, the wind stills, moisture flirts with sprinkles and drizzle, and then raindrops arrive before the downpour. This storm skips the preamble. The footpath fills with running water. Rains soaks my ball cap, clothes, boots, and feet before the day's journey begins. I am grateful the temperature is cool.

The sky drowns the ground we walk on to Atkins, Virginia. Daniel's father picked the wrong weekend to enjoy the Appalachian Trail experience. He arrives in Atkins, today.

I shout my dog's name to gain his attention.

"Hey Buddy, I wonder if the weather has forced Daniel's father to cancel the hike with his son? I hope he still comes to Atkins. Daniel worked hard to prepare for his dad and uncle this weekend. They can still hang-out together. Activity is irrelevant, spending time together matters."

Buddy steps beside me and places his head under my hand.

"You're right, Poppy. I'm here because you're here."

I smile at Buddy's thought and imagine the thrill we'd enjoy riding with Bubba in torrential rain on mountain roads to reach Knot Maul Shelter. Bubba built his late model truck to drive in the mud. If the men stick to their plan, the drive with Bubba on these mountain roads will be special. Father, son, and uncle will create a lifetime memory without leaving the pickup's cab.

Buddy and I ignore our predicament and have fun this morning. I am isolated with nature. I should be melancholy, walking alone in this gray, wet world. Factors beyond my control do not change my mind-set today. I am whole—filled with strength and positive energy. We track a saddle-shaped depression along Brushy Mountain's side. Possum Creek roars with raging water to our right. Rain filters through the tree canopy. Run-off pours through hidden channels on the mountain side to merge with the creek. The waterway thunders as run-off pours over large stones spilling across natural borders.

Dream qualities still fill the atmosphere when we reach Rich Valley's flat ground and cross a wooden bridge near O'Lystery Pavilion. A generous stranger has placed two ice chests beside the wooden bridge we use to cross the swollen stream. A sign attached to the insulated boxes invites trail walkers to help themselves to the contents. Soft drinks occupy one ice chest. Little Debbie's, Honey Buns, and assorted potato chips fill the second ice chest. We may walk by ourselves on this path, but I know we do not walk alone.

Buddy and I step under O'Lystery Pavilion's roof to escape rain and enjoy a stranger's gift. Buddy's backpack is heavy with water-weight when I lift it from his back. I'm glad we removed his food this morning. Buddy can't shake hard enough or long enough to remove the water from his fur.

"Shake, rattle and roll, Buddy-Boy. Are you ready for a treat?" I ask, as I scatter food packages on a picnic table. I fill his water bowl with Sprite and open the Little Debbie and potato chip packages he pulls from the table. When he's finished eating these treats, he helps himself to a Honey Bun.

Buddy's idea is good. I won't shake, rattle, or roll in the pavilion, but I will change clothes and put on my rain gear. My shirt is off when a car filled with people stops on the road beside the pavilion.

"New knowledge, Buddy: never expect privacy when we walk beside a paved road."

A fit woman in her early 50s opens the trunk and removes a daypack and hiking poles. She wears a rain jacket over expensive hiking clothes. When the car drives away, she waves to us, then walks through the rain by herself to the trailhead and begins her hike toward Atkins.

The first step outside the pavilion's cover is the same as stepping into the shower at home: dry to wet with nothing in between. We walk across saturated grass before we cross VA42 and arrive at the trailhead. We stay on Rich Valley's flat ground for a distance, moving across land owned by private owners. I find pleasure in these surroundings. It breaks the routine. We travel in woods and grassland instead of the wilderness. We share open pasture with livestock who call this grassland home.

When the livestock are present, it means fencing and fence crossings are nearby. Two large wood ladders form most crossovers. Each ladder base stands on its side of the fence. The wood tops form a teepee where they meet over the fence. Fence crossing is a nuisance more than a challenge for me. Buddy is a different story. He doesn't climb ladders. We negotiate several fence crossings this morning. I'm glad we don't face a fence Buddy can't crawl under or climb through when I carry his pack.

The lady moves fast on flat farm land and forest floor. I lose visual contact with her as we work through tight switchbacks to climb grade. We meet this impressive person when we cross the Holston River Bridge late this morning. She welcomes us with a pleasant smile. I learn this athlete finished her southbound thruhike many years ago. She returns to the trail now, with family and friends to finish small sections she skipped during the original hike. She mentions she prefers to walk alone. We honor her preference. Buddy and I watch her cross the bridge, then turn our attention to Holston River's rolling current.

The Appalachians are a range of mountains. They span two countries and cross 18 states from Alabama to Maine. For me, the Appalachian Mountains are ground I see between footsteps and pole plants; a series of steep climbs up and down mountain sides. Each ascent presents a unique ridgeline replaced by a descent to a valley. Sharp inclines and declines include a series of switchbacks created to break steep grade into a manageable effort.

The section we come face to face with today replicates our Appalachian Trail experience. We leave Jefferson National Forest to cross Rich Valley, then return to tree cover when Buddy and I cross the Holston River Bridge and step onto Walker Mountain. I'm grateful trail-makers create switchbacks at the mountain's sharpest grades. I'm hungry when we reach the top of Little Brushy Mountain. Nourishment is important, but I'm unwilling to expose my backpack to rain to secure food. When a thick clump of tall brush presents itself on the ridgeline, I crawl under the makeshift shelter and eat lunch with Buddy. When we finish our meal, we start a 900-foot descent to Atkins, Virginia.

I ride my bicycle on difficult grades. The high-speed descent is the reward for the effort I give to reach the top of a steep hill. The balance between physical effort and pleasure makes hill climbing a worthwhile trial.

Hill running resembles hiking on this terrain. The contrast is weight carried and length of time committed to the task. Uphill runs tax stamina. Downhill runs punish my feet, ankles, knees, hips, and lower back.

When I run downhill, my technique determines the speed I sustain, the energy I consume, and the punishment I absorb. If I bend knees and lean backward against grade to descend a hill, I limit the chance of falling. The tradeoff is: I run a slower pace and my body takes a pounding. I descend these mountainsides using this technique carrying a 40-pound backpack. My lower body pays a price each step downhill.

The last year I entered marathons, I ran in Sacramento, California with my friend Jeff Zwiener. The California Marathon is a famous race known for its downhill miles. I know my body. When I signed up for the race, I doubted I could finish the marathon leaning back against the grade.

I prepared for this race by teaching myself to overcome the fear of falling face first while running downhill. When I became confident in my new skill, I changed the way I approach the descents. Instead of leaning back with the brakes on, I lean forward at hill crests. I bend at my ankles instead of my knees, keep my back straight, relax my body, and follow my nose and chest downhill. The experience is exhilarating. Instead of beating up my body, I relax, gain back a normal heart beat, and I change my mind's focus from pain to excitement.

When I changed my approach to descents, I gained speed compared to my competitors and reduced damage to my joints. I finished the California Marathon with a personal best time. As important, I achieved a fair balance between work effort and pleasure running hills.

I have bike handling skills and running skills needed to descend at speeds that thrill me. The risk involved in this effort creates pleasure for me. I don't have the same skill to manage risk wearing a backpack on these mountain paths.

Balance between pleasure and physical effort on the Appalachian Trail does not come from the thrill of the descent. Pleasure comes in the satisfaction I receive, knowing I finish both sides of each climb and I am prepared to start the next climb. I accept the damage I cause to my feet and joints to finish this journey.

We arrive in Atkins, Virginia when the trail delivers us to an open field leading to an interstate highway crossover. Buddy and I are drenched and bitterly cold. I am eager to find dry ground and to find something warm to drink. A 20-minute walk places us inside a Sunoco Convenience Store serving locals and travelers.

The clerk is sympathetic when I enter the establishment. He smiles at me and then he says in a friendly voice:

"Take your dog outside and don't come back in with your equipment."

"Right, I knew that." I apologize, open the door, drop my backpack on the wet sidewalk, and hand Buddy over to a stranger named Benny for the chance to embrace the sound and smell of civilization in warmth. I return to my world a few minutes later, with a steaming cup of coffee and a pack of cigarettes I give to Benny.

My spirit lifts as I glance toward the covered space protecting the gas pumps. Maye waves while she dries Buddy with a blanket. Our trail boss has arrived to keep her date with Buddy-Buddy. It's a nice end to a good second week.

Chapter Nineteen
Partnership Shelter

Mt. Rogers Visitor Center is a short hike from Atkins Virginia. Partnership Shelter is a stone's throw from the visitor center. The shelter is a two-story log cabin that can hold up 16 people, and includes a water faucet, a shower, and a laundry sink.

Buddy and I are first to arrive this afternoon. Since we are early, I fill my water bottles at the laundry sink and decide to set aside my evening chores. I toss my pack on the shelter floor without declaring a sleeping space. I investigate the shelter's amenities and visit the Mt. Rogers Visitor Center. Buddy explores the perimeter looking for playmates.

Today has been hard. The sky is gloomy with heavy rain clouds. My mind cycles thoughts matching the clouds overhead. I exhaust positive ways to occupy my brain and give in to a melancholy mood. Buddy must sense my change in emotions. He returns to the picnic table and lies next to my feet.

When you live in isolation, you endure countless hours, considering relationships and events that shape you and limit you as a person. Most are whispers from past life; memories I cultivate outside the conscious reach of daily thought.

Reliving deep memories hurts. Active participation in backcountry's physical hardship does not mask the painful emotions I nurture from a time long gone. My inner-voice cycles these thoughts until I move past my truth to discover truth from everyone's viewpoint without prejudice. Understanding reality from other's perspective does not heal me, but it does lead to awareness, acceptance, and refreshing peace. The challenge waiting my return to civilization is this: do not clothe new life with past results or future hopes.

Buddy rises from the ground to stand by me. I know his thoughts:

"*Poppy, are you okay? What are you churning through now?*"

"Hey Sweet-Boy. Everything is fine, just sad this afternoon. I'm contemplating deep stuff," I say with a chuckle, attempting to break my gloomy mindset. "I am searching for a healthy way to live without carrying harmful emotions. Consider this with me, Big-Boy."

Buddy accepts my invitation and leans forward, resting his chin on my thigh.

Daily living resembles adults playing a child's ballgame. The game is played with a passion that can turn into anger. Teams compete with rough and tumble aggression. Players exchange harsh words without thought. They expect disputes in keeping with unspoken rules. We experience similar emotions competing for individual space at home, school, work, and a bedroom behind closed doors.

"Buddy, most players keep focused, even if the competitors aren't behaving in a sportsmanlike fashion. They give their best efforts playing through a competitor's poor behavior, then walk away before returning to begin a new play. They know angry words are empty chatter," I say aloud, breaking the campground silence.

Fans, umpires, and players play their role and receive their reward. Players leave the playing field when a batter makes the final out. Fans go after the players and the coaches leave. The grounds crew exits when the stadium is clean, and the field is prepared for tomorrow's game. Owners realize no one wants to sit in yesterday's mess, watching today's game.

Three hours ago, the stadium rocked with competitive energy and an exciting aura. Now, the stadium is clean, and the ballpark is empty. Players, coaches, umpires, press, fans, stadium employees are gone.

No mulligan is offered. Today is finished.

Was a game played today? I ask myself. Yes, the scoreboard reports the final score and competitive emotions linked to success, discomfort, personal wrongs, and private disappointments keep the game alive for me when no one exists to replay the game.

I scratch my dog's head and rub his ears before I speak again.

"Buddy-Boy, this will matter when my day is over. Did I act with honor today and give the best of my ability? Did I make amends when I didn't? This is my challenge each night: relive the game, good plays, fouls, and errors without considering the final score. Embrace good plays and learn from poor plays without excuse. When I'm finished, stack the behavior and the emotions in a pile and leave them for yesterday. IAM will discard them where she chooses.

"Will you please help me remember this, Buddy? Start fresh each new day. Nobody wants to live in yesterday's mess, engaging today's opportunities."

Buddy smiles and rises on his back haunches. He places his forelegs around my waist and places his block head on my chest as if to say, *"Poppy, I love you. I'll give you my best. You are a stubborn, prideful man. Will you listen when I remind you?"*

I laugh at my perceptive companion.

"I'll give you my best, Buddy."

Melancholy's bubble bursts with adrenaline's fear. I'm startled back to reality by a dog's vicious growl as an angry man screams at me:

"Get control of your dog."

Get control of my dog? I stand up and walk into the open, ignoring Buddy, who is now standing by my side. This is my fight. The man has picked the wrong person to scream at this afternoon. I'm in no mood for this behavior, today. I stare at the man and his dog with a hard gaze I seldom present.

The man changes his tone, but still demands I get control of Buddy. I do not change my stance or my glare. I have no intentions of uttering a word to this rude mountain-man. My dog is under control. He is standing by my side, ready to respond with courtesy or aggression.

The man lowers his voice to a calm tone and requests I place Buddy on his lead.

The stranger's trail name is "Lone Wolf". His home is Tennessee. I place Buddy on his lead, then listen to Lone Wolf's chatter for a few minutes. I have worked with intense people throughout my career. Folks say I am direct when a problematic situation warrants keen focus. Lone Wolf raises intensity to a new level.

I'm glad I stayed quiet and listened. This Tennessean is rough, but his intentions are honorable.

At 4:15 pm, I decide it will be a long and unpleasant night if we stay together at the shelter. I glance at the dark rain clouds, throw on our packs, and head for the next shelter; which is 10-miles away. When I reach the campsite perimeter, I pause and turn to look at Lone Wolf. He smiles and walks toward us.

"Jimmy Doug, take my phone number. Water is scarce where I live. I'll be happy to bring you and Buddy bottled water, and I will be happy to drive you to the next section of the AT that has water. You call me, and we will figure it out together."

This is Lone Wolf's friendship offer. What can I say, but "thank you"? I wave, smile, and then Buddy and I leave without eating our supper. I'm grateful I filled my water bottles when I arrived at Partnership Shelter.

We aren't on the trail 30-minutes before the sky opens and pours rain on us.

"What can I do, Buddy?"

My dog looks at me through the rain.

"This was your decision, Poppy. That man and dog were pure bark. The dog and I were becoming friends. Now, put on your rain suit, change from hiking boots to trail running shoes, secure your headlamp, and let's get moving."

"You are right Buddy, I reacted without considering the situation. It was a poor decision."

Before I realize what is happening, the rain intensifies, the temperature drops, and the forest turns pitch-black. The Appalachian Trail's pathway is easy to follow from one location to another during dawn, daylight, and dusk hours. Buddy leads without the aid of the white blaze trail markers whenever he chooses. I will learn when I turn northbound, it's pleasant to navigate in the dark when the night sky is transparent. This is not a bright night.

"Buddy, 40-years have passed since I navigated new terrain in these conditions. We will get through this predicament if we work together. I'll focus on the trail markers. You track hiker scent. We'll be okay. If we lose the way, we will camp where we stand until the sun rises. Let's see what we still have in us, Big Boy!"

Abysmal conditions in daylight are special tonight. Body heat escapes through my raincoat's vents and open collar. Body temperature blends with cold rain to produce steam. Warm breath mixed with the cold night air creates vapor. Vapor isn't new; it forms and dissipates without causing a distraction in daylight. My headlamp struggles to penetrate the mist that shrouds us and the rain that covers us. It's same as driving a car through fog with the car lights switched to high beam.

White trail markers created with reflective paint are helpful but not perfect in these conditions. Buddy works hard to track the trail on the ground I do not see. Despite our best effort, we still lose our way three times. We are lucky tonight. *We are so lucky.* The footpath finds us each time we retrace our steps.

Buddy is the first to arrive at the side trail leading to Trimpi Shelter. My watch reads 10:00 pm. My dog walks to the shelter without waiting for permission. He waits in the cold rain for me to arrive.

Steam lifts off Buddy when my headlamp illuminates him staring into Trimpi's dark open face. My heart sinks when my light penetrates the shelter's contents. The shelter is full. I can't believe we hiked this far, in these conditions, to pitch a tent in the pouring rain.

Buddy's not sleeping under a tent flap with his torso exposed to the elements. He jumps onto the elevated floor before I can stop his forward momentum. This time, my headlamp illuminates two sleeping hikers surrounded by wet clothes and scattered equipment. I am uncomfortable disturbing these people, but grateful Buddy has no intention of sleeping in the rain.

Daniel and Jordan raise their heads from inside their sleeping bags. We are safe, and we are with friends. I sit on the shelter floor and give Buddy a hug before I take off his pack. Buddy returns my love and shared relief. He nuzzles his wet body against me before he shares his opinion of tonight's experience:

"Poppy you did well tonight. Thank you for staying close. It's a good thing Daniel and Jordan left a scent to follow."

Buddy may be right. He is an excellent tracker.

Daniel is kind to us. He rises and moves his sleeping bag to the loft so that Buddy and I have a warm place to rest beside each other. We don't eat tonight, but we sleep well.

Tears surface recalling my walk with my dog from Partnership Shelter to Trimpi Shelter, today. This magnificent animal lies by my writing table while I tell you our story. Lone Wolf is not the last time I react in frustration. I am blessed to still have Simpson's Buddy-Boy by my side, quietly leading the way.

Chapter Twenty
Trimpi Shelter

Mt. Rogers National Recreation Area hosts 60-miles of Appalachian Trail. We started this trek last night. We are rarely alone. Tourists and weekend hikers offer friendly energy and welcome acts of kindness. Buddy and I watch the recreation area test city legs on spirited rock climbs at Fatman Squeeze, Wilburn Ridge, and outings to the two highest peaks in Virginia: Mt. Rogers at 5,728-feet and Whitetop Mountain at 5,518-feet.

Anyone with a week vacation, and a keen interest in testing the Appalachian Trail for the first time, should consider the walk from the NRA Welcome Center to Damascus, Virginia.

Here are factors to consider before you post this bucket list target on the refrigerator door: are you afraid of the dark? Can you tolerate pooping in an outhouse, wearing the same clothing for days, and bathing once a week? Most importantly, can you tote a 40-pound backpack while you climb rock structures, ascend and descend rolling changes in grade, and avoid tree roots, muddy stream beds, and rocks of different sizes and shapes?

If these factors sound like a fun challenge, I encourage you to prepare and try. You will enjoy similar discoveries Buddy and I share this coming week.

Today is September 26, 2013. We've hiked for thirteen days and have covered 140 miles since Adam delivered us to the Catawba, Virginia Trailhead.

Professor is a distinguished mentor at Baylor Law School. He is an experienced mountain climber and backcountry walker. We became friends when we hiked the Chilkoot Trail in Alaska and part of the Appalachian Trail in North Carolina. I've gained valuable knowledge observing Professor on our trips.

The morning after we climbed through the icy mist to summit Chilkoot Pass and cross the Canadian Border, I stood by Professor in damp clothes drinking hot coffee.

"Professor, my shirt and pants are moist. How did you dry your clothes without a fire last night?"

"Simple, Jimmy Doug. I wear my clothes while I sleep in my sleeping bag."

BS or truth, I didn't care when I climbed into my sleeping bag wearing wet clothes last night.

When the sun was rising this morning, the sleeping bag zippers heralded the start of a new hiking day. Buddy and I rise first. We have no choice. I block the path from Daniel's sleeping perch to the floor.

My clothes are dry. I pull my boots out of the waterproof bag. My boots are dry. No reason to focus on my trail running shoes. I will tie them to my backpack, so they can dry out in the morning sun. I am ready for today; comfortable and grateful we survived last night's hike.

"Buddy, are you hungry?" I ask, while I rub his shoulders, back, and hips. My dog's body shakes in rhythm with his tail wag. He's hungry. I need to get moving!

I sense friction between my two trail friends. Few words are spoken between the two hiking companions. I'm pleased to see Jordan yet surprised this young thru-hiker is still walking with Daniel.

"Jordan, I thought you were picking up your re-supply package in Atkins and returning to the trail?"

Jordan looks up from his chores.

"I was. My family paid a surprise visit. Mom and Dad drove from Pennsylvania to Atkins to take me shopping at the Outfitter in Damascus, Virginia. Check out my new coat, Jimmy Doug."

"Nice jacket, Jordan. Why are you organizing your equipment in my backpack?" I ask with a tone of false concern.

Jordan stops working, speaks, and then pauses. We both smile when he realizes I am teasing. Jordan bought the same backpack as mine this weekend.

"Daniel, thanks again for making space for us last night. I apologize for creating the disturbance."

"No problem, Jimmy Doug. We're glad you made it to the shelter. I was happy to move. I love Buddy-Boy, but you can sleep next to your wet dog."

Buddy's tail wags. He accepts Daniel's words as a compliment. We laugh when Buddy crosses the floor to lick Daniel's hand.

"Hey Daniel, Buddy and I tramped through the rain most of the way to Atkins, Friday. It rained this weekend. Did you cancel the hike with your father and uncle?"

Daniel looks at me with twinkling eyes.

"Daniel, did you hike with your father in this weather?" I ask again, with a surprised tone.

"We did, Jimmy Doug. Dad and Uncle got drenched on the trail, but finished their hike as planned. Dad prepared and did well. Uncle carried 70 pounds of every treat you can imagine. He kept us supplied at the shelter and back at the motel when we finished."

"I know your father was proud."

Daniel is quiet for a moment.

"Dad was affirming. He communicated his appreciation for what we are up against out here."

I can tell Daniel wants to share more with me but doesn't.

Jordan steps forward to interject himself back into the conversation.

"Jimmy Doug, why were you out past your bedtime?"

I smile at Jordan and present a brief explanation of our clash with Lone Wolf at Partnership Shelter and the nuances we experienced hiking in the rain last night. Based on our shelter mates' tone of voice and body language, Simpson's Buddy-Boy and I have earned a level of respect.

Buddy and I walk away from Trimpi Shelter to start our hiking day when Jordan grabs his baby-wipes and heads for the outhouse. Daniel sits at the picnic table. He's preoccupied with reading from a heavy book he stores in his backpack. Daniel closes the large book as we pass.

"What are you reading?" I ask, pointing to the book he opens again.

"It's a Buddhist Bible I found in the drop box at Partnership Shelter."

"I've never chatted with a Siddhartha Gautama follower. What are you contemplating?"

Daniel relaxes when he hears my question. He sees from my expression, I have a genuine interest hearing his response.

"I'm not a Buddhist, Jimmy Doug. Just curious. I'm struggling to understand my first reading. Any chance you might understand what Buddha is communicating in this passage?"

"I don't know, Daniel. I'm not a Buddhist, either. Gautama Buddha was a wise man. I doubt he gained wisdom remaining in isolation, scribing words onto paper channeled to him by a celestial entity. I'm confident Buddha earned the truth you consider honoring life failures interacting with people from different backgrounds, cultures, and religions. We have the same opportunity to earn our truth. Share with me what you are working on, so I can comprehend."

I respect Daniel for taking time to outline his thoughts. He shares instruction that encourages people to find contentment in every circumstance of life: never judge a person and always run from evil. Buddy and I listen to Daniel while he labors to decipher the conflicting ideas presented to him in the literature.

I shake my head from side to side and smile when Daniel lifts his eyes from the book.

"Was I talking in my sleep last night, Daniel? No kidding, I've pondered similar thoughts for days."

Jordan arrives at the picnic table with a light step and a smile.

"No Jimmy Doug. You don't talk in your sleep. You hold your breath," Jordan teases.

I smile at Jordan, acknowledging this well-known truth.

"Guys, I have to tell you: I wasn't expecting to stand with smart men from New Jersey and Pennsylvania, on a mountain in Southern Virginia; wearing a 40-pound backpack and discussing philosophy. How did I get so lucky?"

"Jimmy Doug, you've earned the opportunity with the gray beard covering your face," Daniel responds, laughing at his own humor.

I smile at my friend.

"Daniel, you've picked a hard but important lesson to understand and apply. I congratulate you for the solid logic you used to outline why Gautama's teaching smashes against daily existing. Most people reject this truth. For them, true contentment is unattainable in this life, let alone in every situation. They see these words as an ideal reserved for life after this lifetime, or religious theology established for monks, cloistered nuns, and new age cult members set apart from the world."

"Here's what I know today: If I seek truth the way a pit bull dog takes to a meat bone or a tire hanging from a rope in the garage, I will find truth; the same as Buddha discovered his truth in this passage.

"The Originator of Life Lessons does not keep secrets locked in a steel vault stored in mystic space. She wants to share everything with her creation but waits to gain a person's full attention before she does. The good news is: you've still got the states of Tennessee, North Carolina, and Georgia to traverse in solitude before you return to civilization. I'm confident you will discover how this teaching can serve as a cornerstone for practical living when you start the next phase of life."

"Jimmy Doug, that's a copout. I want to hear your opinion."

"No, Daniel. It's not a copout. Seek your own truth. If you care and you pay close attention to your inner-voice in life's wilderness, you can filter through other beliefs and discover your truth.

"How I model my beliefs and actions to please others determines whose truth I trust and whose life I live. For me, the copout is thinking I must rely on religious doctrine or other people's opinions to gain wisdom and discover life truth. That mindset has been my greatest failure."

"I agree with you, Daniel. Happiness, joy and even euphoria are emotions that exist for me in temporary places where I seek to mask chaos filtering throughout my life. Peace and security seldom attach to those emotions. Consider this with me: Gautama is not challenging me to be happy, joyful, or euphoric in every turn of events. We live through the full emotional gambit for a reason; we are alive and engaged. He challenges me to be satisfied where I stand, and at peace and secure in the strength and integrity that lives in me in every situation; good, hard, and mundane.

"Guys, strength and integrity that transcends circumstance lives in my soul, not my body or my mind. Souls exist without the reference to people's religious performance or comprehension. I choose for myself whether I follow my inner-voice to be content, or I listen to body and mind and live a closed life in an insecure world. I receive truth if I listen to my inner-voice without bias. How I use truth is my choice."

When I finish expressing my opinion, Jordan rubs Buddy's head and moves toward the shelter.

Daniel smiles and gets up from the bench to give me a hug.

"Thanks, Jimmy Doug. We'll talk again."

Jordan passes us on the trail 20-minutes later. Daniel follows an hour later.

"What's up with those two, Buddy?"

"I don't know, Poppy," Buddy responds, glancing toward me then picking up the pace to climb the incline Daniel just ascended.

Buddy and I enjoy hours of solitude. We move in cadence with the familiar rhythm of moderate ascents, followed by longer descents; and then we start again. My walking trance fades when a good water source presents itself.

I lean over a handrail on a wooden bridge to watch Buddy drink and frolic in the mountain spring. Waves of thru-hikers adorned in iPods blow by us in mass. I assume the last group of southbound through hikers have arrived. Admiration for their effort grows. Sadness replaces excitement as I notice goal-driven athletes exchange solitude's lifetime gifts to embrace social awareness.

These young athletes are distinctive. My dog could hike with these people. If I jogged, I might keep up with their walking pace. They carry minimal backpacks, wear low cut trail running shoes, and dress in running shorts and t-shirts.

A few descend the stream embankment to capture drinking water. They ignore Buddy's friendly greeting. The focused youth bend their knees to squat, then scoop water with their bottle. Thirsty, they drink from the stream I filtered water from several minutes earlier.

Several hikers wave hellos, smile without making eye contact, and then burst across the bridge. These extraordinary youngsters see the bridge's wooden frame as an obstacle to cross. I view the bridge and envision people from times past transport supplies and equipment over rugged terrain to make strangers' lives easier. I accept their selfless work as a gift and appreciate the standing art.

Most trail warriors are half my age. We share ground and accomplish the same task. Many are present for a different reason than me. These people hike the Appalachian Trail to prove themselves. They compete with self and peer to finish walking the entire Appalachian Trail before moving on to the next life challenge.

I wonder if they recognize the sound of silence on this trail. Can they distinguish their inner-voice surrounded by this crowd and the frantic pace they sustain? Will they discover life-freeing truths found in solitude or barrel through this experience and return to life's chaos to bulldoze through a lifetime of experiences? Will I follow their lead, again? Time will measure these young men, the same as it measured me. I lived my life the way these men are attacking the Appalachian Trail. I know now, time is not infinite. It is finite. How I live each day matters. Will it be on scorched earth or planted ground?

The embankment is quiet now. The thundering herd has vacated these woods. Water moves beneath the bridge, spilling its contents from a terraced ledge into the sun-glazed stream pooling below our feet.

"How does a Snickers bar sound, Buddy?"

Buddy stands at attention, waiting for me to remove the wrapper before we take turns eating from the candy bar.

When we finish our snack, I speak softly.

"Come here Sweet-Boy," I say to Buddy, as I sit on the embankment by his side. My Labrador lays his big block head in my lap while I brush his white hair with my fingers.

I am still in deep thought when Buddy stands and bolts across the stream embankment. I see why my dog is excited. An elite southbound thru-hiker has arrived at the bridge carrying a Jack Russell Terrier. Buddy has a new friend.

James extends the courtesy expected from a seasoned backcountry walker. He offers his hand in greeting then says, "Don't get up, sir. Do you mind me sitting with you while my dog and I eat lunch?"

James shares typical thru-hiker characteristics. He is bright, educated, curious, and athletic. James is present to prove himself to himself. He has an older brother who joined the U.S. Army as an officer and served in Iraq. James has chosen the Appalachian Trail instead of the military to begin life his way.

James has reached the point in his journey where he is struggling with isolation. Buddy and I stay and share the lunch break with this young man from the Washington D.C. locality.

It's interesting to see James unload his backpack to gather his food. His contents are distinct from Daniel's, Jordan's, Ray's, and mine. James gives up equipment and extra clothes to cut weight and carry the quantity of food he and his dog need to replace the many calories they burn every day.

"Jimmy Doug, what are your plans for Buddy when you reach the Smokey Mountains?"

"I haven't given the Smokey Mountains much consideration, James. Buddy is gaining strength. I'm sure he will be fine walking with me. Why do you ask?"

"It's against the law to bring dogs on the trail in the Smokey Mountain National Park."

"Are you kidding me? Will the dog police throw me or Buddy in jail if they catch me walking with my dog across the mountains?" I ask James with a smile on my face.

"Who knows, Jimmy Doug? Maybe you will both go to jail," James responds with his own humor. "I'm not willing to find out. I hear jail's no fun and the fine can be more money than I have available."

"What a mess. What are your plans for Jack Russell, James?"

James shares his options for Jack Russell while he consumes peanut butter and honey sandwiches. By the time James finishes lunch, I'm convinced Buddy and I have a problem. Damascus, Virginia is a short distance from our present location. The Great Smokey Mountain National Park is 200 miles from Damascus, Virginia.

I watch James and Jack Russell pack their belongings and cross the bridge before I pull out *The Thru-Hikers' Companion*.

"Buddy, listen to this. James is right. The guidebook says dogs are not permitted in the park. The fine is up to $500. One dog hostel offers to pick up, board, and deliver for $250."

Buddy sits, staring into my eyes.

"What do you think, Buddy? Do you want to stay at a dog-hotel while I hike the Great Smokey Mountain National Park?"

Buddy leaves no doubt what he is thinking.

"Poppy, I go where you go. Do you want to stay at a dog hotel?"

My dog's right. We will work around this inconvenience.

Chapter Twenty-One
Damascus Virginia

Hurricane Mountain earns my respect for its beauty and challenging terrain. We hike nine miles, climb 2,200-feet, and drop 1,400-feet to arrive at the mountain's shelter. Two weeks ago, this ascent would crush me. Today, I'm hungry.

I pull out my cell phone at the intersection where the side trail to the shelter meets the Appalachian Trail. There is a faint connection.

"Hey Buddy, we can call Sissy from a higher elevation. Do you want to climb this side trail and eat a snack at the shelter?"

My dog jogs by me with his tail wagging when I make the turn onto the new path and start the short ascent to the shelter campsite. When I arrive, Buddy is playing chase with Jack Russell. I wave to James, show him my cell phone, and walk away to find a strong signal to call my daughter.

Lacey answers on the second ring.

"Hi Daddy. I hoped you'd call this week. Have you followed the news? Our freshman senator, Ted Cruz, has denounced Obamacare on the Senate Floor this week. He's arguing for a government shutdown, unless President Obama agrees to defund the Affordable Care Act. We know the president will never agree to abandon his healthcare legislation."

"If Senator Cruz gets his way, there's a good chance President Obama will retaliate."

"Dad, the president might close the national parks."

I'm stunned. Reality sets in faster than my mind can respond. We have four to six weeks of hiking weather available to finish out this year. Buddy isn't allowed to enter the Smokey Mountains. Now, I may be blocked from hiking this magnificent national treasure on my own. Even if they catch me and extricate the fine, I cannot afford the time loss sitting at Dolly Parton

World; waiting for Congress and the Whitehouse to quit fighting and govern.

"Dad, are you still on the phone?"

"Yes, honey. Just considering a proper response."

"Dad, you can't ignore this fight in Washington, DC. I've researched this for you. National Parks require a permit to hike the backcountry. You can't buy a permit if they close the Smokey Mountain National Park. The fine is up to $5,000 if you get caught violating this rule. What do you think, Daddy?"

Buddy stands by my side now.

"Do we have a choice? I'll set the Smokey Mountains aside for now. When we reach Damascus, Virginia, we will secure transportation to Springer Mountain, Georgia, and head north on the Appalachian Trail until we reach the Smokey Mountain National Park. Hopefully, the government will serve its citizens by the time we arrive at the southern boundary of the national park. I'll get my permit and take my chances with Buddy. We haven't seen a park ranger since we started our journey. I hope the park service hasn't stationed every ranger in the Smokey Mountains."

I can't help but laugh remembering 'Wrong-Way', and other poor choices I've made on this trip.

"Lacey, with my luck, a ranger exists at every shelter. What is the drive time between Texas to Tennessee? The dog-hostel will be tight quarters for Buddy-Boy and me."

Lacey laughs with me and then adds:

"Daddy, I can't get off work to bail you out. Best send your 'Blackhawk-Down' message on Spot if Buddy gets caught. Dr. Zwiener, Mr. Cohen, and Judge Wiser will mobilize resources to rescue you. Please let me know how dog-treats and canned dog food tastes when you get home."

"Okay, thanks for hearing me out. I have a plan. Hopefully, Maye will meet me in Damascus and drive me to Springer Mountain. I'll hike Georgia and North Carolina, skip the Smokey Mountains, and finish the fall hiking season backpacking from Roanoke Virginia to Harper's Ferry, West Virginia. I'll head north from Harper's Ferry to Baxter Peak in the spring, then finish my thru-hike in the Smokey Mountain National Park.

Buddy smiles and scratches my leg when I finish the conversation. It's his way to say, *"Good plan, Poppy. It's good to have a plan."*

"Right, Buddy. We will see how this strategy works for us," I say, patting my dog on the shoulders before we return to the shelter to greet James and eat a snack.

I am pleased James elects to walk with us when we leave Hurricane Mountain Shelter. Old Orchard Shelter is now our target destination.

"Four more miles, Buddy-Boy. I hope your food has settled. We face a 450-foot climb the first mile, then we drop 760-feet to reach the Fox Creek Trailhead before we climb to Old Orchard Shelter. Put on your knee braces."

Buddy gets the joke. He smiles, then heads downhill with Jack Russell to begin the afternoon walk. I spot an excellent camp site beside a running creek two miles from the shelter. Given the number of thru-hikers passing us today, it's safe to assume the shelter will be full when we arrive. This site is much more appealing than pitching my tent beside a crowded shelter. The setting is secluded, and Buddy can play in the stream.

"James, are you camping at the shelter tonight?" I ask while we watch Buddy and Jack Russell drink from Fox Creek.

"The shelter is not my first choice, Jimmy Doug. I'm not a big fan of crowds. I'll find a place to camp beside the trail. What are your plans?"

"The same," I respond.

James and I appreciate the amenities Fox Creek offers this evening. Since we both value the setting, neither one of us will speak up to take the space. James relents when I convince him I need to put in extra miles to shorten tomorrow's hike.

Fox Creek is a 10-minute walk to VA603, and the Fox Creek Trailhead feeding Old Orchard Shelter, Grayson Highlands State Park, and Mt. Rogers. When we arrive at the gravel parking lot supporting the trailhead, a new Suburban is easing into the last available parking space.

Buddy-Boy and I pause when two men in their early forties exit the vehicle's front doors. The males wear do-rags, shorts, and muscle shirts. Two women exit from the passenger doors. The ladies are dressed for country club golf. An older man wearing hiking clothes follows the ladies from the vehicle. The elderly gentleman promptly moves to the back of the Suburban. He secures a backpack and hiking poles and walks toward the trail without so much as waving 'goodbye' to the two couples.

Buddy and I stop to watch the younger adults. The couples move around the vehicle, opening, and closing doors, messing with equipment, and chatting. No one makes a move to place a pack on their back and start toward the trailhead.

"Buddy, I can't decide whether these people are afraid to start the hike, or they are clueless about how to put on their backpacks."

I laugh when one lady pulls out her suitcase. I surprise myself when I say, "Ma'am, best leave the suitcase in the SUV. It is easier to walk a trail when you place hiking poles in each hand."

She laughs at my humor and returns my friendly smile.

"Oh, I know. I'll wear these clothes at the resort my husband is taking me to when we finish this hike."

"Sounds like a fair trade. Have fun and be careful. I'll see you on the trail," I reply, as I wave goodbye to the group.

A mile passes before Buddy and I catch the older gentlemen. He has trained for today. He has no problem climbing the grade and carrying on a lively conversation. I learn he is 82-years-old. When this man was 67-years-old, he walked from Springer Mountain, Georgia to Katahdin, Maine. When he finished his thru-hike, he promised to take his granddaughter for a walk on the Appalachian Trail. He is keeping his promise to her now.

We separate from the gentleman when he slows his pace to wait for his group. This man leaves an impression. He is older than my father. He is here, introducing his family to nature and setting an example for his children, grandchildren, and great grandchildren.

"Buddy, let's do our best to follow in his footsteps with our family."

Buddy picks up the pace, inching away from me on the steep grade. He must smell Daniel and Jordan's scent. He doesn't stop this evening until he finds his friends at the campsite. Daniel is setting up a tent I have never seen. Jordan is preparing a hammock with a cover I did not know he owned.

Weekend hikers fill the campsite. I set up my new, ultra-lite tent at the campsite edge while Buddy greets our neighbors. It is fun to sit back and enjoy everyone, especially when Daniel pulls out his ukulele and jams with another fella playing a harmonica. The campsite feels the same as a neighborhood block party.

Campers drop by my tent to ask questions, share a story, and offer food or drink.

Buddy is a big hit. He is on his own this evening. Daniel, Jordan, and I keep an eye out for my dog, but it's not needed. Everyone loves Buddy.

I fall asleep with an active community at play. I wake with Buddy's head and shoulders stuck inside the tent flap next to me and his body lying under the tent fly that shields our equipment from moisture. A remnant of campers remains at the campsite.

When I complete my morning tasks, Daniel stands alone in the open campground with his backpack resting against a rock. His big book rests on the rock. Buddy and I watch Daniel for a moment. He is in a meditation trance, completing a sequence of yoga poses. Hidden treasures gather to shape Daniel from New Jersey. We leave the campsite without disturbing our friend.

Buddy-Boy and I arrive in Damascus, Virginia Sunday afternoon at the trailhead where US58 meets the Virginia Creeper Trail. We have hiked 16-days, covered 51,000-feet in absolute elevation, and have traveled 185-miles on the Appalachian Trail.

We sit under a shade tree next to a parking lot crammed with vehicles used by bicyclists, runners, hikers, and picnicking families who walk the Appalachian Trail or ride bikes on the Virginia Creeper Trail. I take a healthy dose of Ibuprofen, affectionately known as 'Vitamin I', and hope a local family will approach us to offer a ride to town. There's no chance that will happen. Since hitchhiking is not in our future, I call a cab service for a ride to a local motel to wait for Maye. She changed her work schedule to meet us in Damascus and drive us to Georgia, Tuesday.

Lacey's prediction is right. When I turn on the television this morning, the national park systems are closed to visitors: dogs and people. Fortunately, Buddy and I aren't forced to break the law. Maye has helped solve our problem. Ted Cruz and Barack Obama can entertain America's extreme population boundaries on CNN, FOX News, and MSNBC. Buddy and I will be at Georgia's Amicalola Falls State Park this afternoon, preparing to climb Springer Mountain; the Appalachian Trail's southern terminus.

Chapter Twenty-Two
Springer Mountain Georgia

The Lodge at Amicalola Falls State Park sits in the Chattahoochee National Forest, nine miles from Springer Mountain. Maye pulls her SUV into the parking lot across from the lodge mid-afternoon and helps us unload. Once we have our packs on our backs, Buddy and I follow Maye across the street to the hotel lobby.

The lodge has nice amenities. I assume the manager is approaching to welcome us and offer his help during our visit. But not today.

"Sir, animals must stay on a leash. Is that understood?"

"Yes, I understand," I reply with a polite tone.

I smile when Buddy extends a paw to shake the man's hand. "Please accept my apology. I left my manners in the woods," I say to the manager as Maye moves to the registrar desk to secure a room while I find Buddy's lead and attach it to his collar. When I glance up, I can tell by Maye's body language and facial expression I have a bigger problem than walking through the lodge with Buddy on a lead.

Maye returns a few minutes later with a key in her hand.

"Is everything okay, Maye?"

"No, Jimmy Doug. Let's go outside and talk. I made a decision you may not appreciate."

Maye is quiet as we walk to a park bench stationed in a floral garden. Buddy finds a soft spot to lay once we sit.

"Jimmy Doug, Buddy's strong and happy. He's had a great hike to this point. The next 300-miles is more difficult. If Buddy goes with you today, I'm concerned his body will break down and he will never recover."

Maye's concern is valid. I listen to her with soft eyes and rub Buddy's shoulders without speaking.

"Jimmy Doug, things happen for a reason. At this point, it's important to pay attention and accept the message. I want you to consider our predicament today. We've driven from Damascus Virginia to Springer Mountain, Georgia because dogs aren't allowed in the Smoky Mountains.

"Jimmy Doug, this lodge does not allow animals in its guest rooms. I purchased a room for you, tonight. Here's your room key and free breakfast coupon. I'm taking Buddy home with me."

I slide from the park bench and hold my 105-pound Labrador Retriever. A sad smile crosses my face and I nod my head as a 'yes'. Maye is right. I appreciate her strength and her friendship.

"Buddy-Boy, thank you for leading me from Kansas to Springer Mountain. You've kept me safe every step. I'm strong now. I'd be happy if you'd take a break and get ready for the next trek coming our way. Will you please take Maye home? Keep her safe while I hike Georgia, North Carolina, and Northern Virginia to Maryland. Sleep on your new bed, enjoy the great memories we share, eat healthy food, and drink water from a faucet. Wait for me and we will go home together when I finish at Harper's Ferry in November."

Buddy continues to lay his head in my lap while I stroke his fur. I can tell he's thinking, because his tail is thumping the ground. Once he's ready, he rises from the ground to face me. He licks my face, then rests his head on my shoulder.

"Buddy, you're the finest dog that's ever lived. I love you, too," I whisper in my best friend's ear.

Once Buddy shares his decision with me and hugs me goodbye, he walks to Maye's SUV and sits by the cargo door. He's ready for a vacation.

The approach trail from Amicalola Falls State Park to Springer Mountain holds a special status. This path is the start of an odyssey for northbound adventure seekers and the end of a physical and emotional journey for southbound thru-hikers.

Southbound thru-hikers float over the trail surface to finish their last 8.8-miles. Newcomers head north battling equipment, terrain, and elevation to finish their first day at a shelter near the southern terminus. I wonder how many thru-hiker dreams shatter before newcomers reach the Appalachian Trail.

Today is my 17th hiking day. I'm not starting an adventure and I'm not finishing a journey—except I am in a way. I hike by myself now. It's one thing to be alone with your dog, it's another to be lonely. I miss my dog, my family, and my friends. Maybe I need a vacation.

I hike the approach trail to the Appalachian Trail lost in melancholic thought. This isn't good. When I find a cell phone connection, I call Leah Jackson, a hiking and marathon running partner. She always cuts through my whining and knows the right words to motivate me. After brief small talk, I get right to the point:

"Leah, I left Buddy behind when I headed north at Springer Mountain. Hiking solo for the rest of this journey is an intimidating prospect."

"Doug, solitude is the heart of your journey. Buddy walked with a purpose. Wilderness is now your constant companion. You have much to learn and explore between Springer Mountain, Georgia, and Harper's Ferry, West Virginia. Listen closely. Once your eyes focus on your surroundings instead of your situation, your mind will open to beauty that photographs cannot depict and words cannot describe."

"Thank you, Leah."

"You're welcome, friend. Call me often and please keep emailing your pictures. Your photography is beautiful."

Leah is right. If I focus on my circumstances, I will fight emotional turmoil until I walk off the Appalachian Trail. I can finish what I start today if I concentrate on my surroundings and enjoy every opportunity.

I appreciate the fact the approach trail packs a punch. One moment, I struggle to climb this mountainside. The next step the foliage parts and I enter surreal space celebrating my arrival at The Appalachian National Scenic Trail Southern Terminus.

An aura of hope and triumph fills this mountaintop. I take off my backpack and boots and bask in this special energy left by thousands who started or finished personal journeys atop Springer Mountain. I stay here until daylight turns to dusk. When I leave to set up camp at Springer Mountain Shelter, I share my predecessor's dream to finish my trek in solitude at Katahdin Mountain: the Appalachian Trail's northern terminus.

Chapter Twenty-Three
Albert Mountain Fire Tower, North Carolina

My arm brushes against a sharp bush, waking me from a walking trance. This distraction is a welcome gift. I need to be alert. A complicated stream crossing sits at the bottom of the ravine I am traversing.

Kirby Creek differs from other water crossings I've addressed this week. A strong current emerges between steep walls at the far end of the ravine. Deep pools of transparent water form and separate at different focal points. I had better think this through or I will take a cold bath wearing a full backpack. The setting is tranquil to view. Crossing with dry equipment will be a challenge.

It is early afternoon and the next shelter, Carter Gap, is a short walk from this stream. I'm not pressed for time, so I sit and ponder this intersection. Small boulders outline the creek edge. Two sit side-by-side, making a natural table and chair. I take off my backpack and make myself comfortable.

Water flows in a channel on a rock bed formed by the ravine. Steady current transforms to small pockets of quiet water. The overflow rolls around or slides over many of the big rocks I need to step on to cross over this waterway. The creek deposits part of its volume into other pools before the fast water joins up with sister currents to rush downstream to Nantahala River.

I walk in a natural sanctuary every day. Magnificent views are the norm. This setting is rare by those standards. I sit on my rock, boiling water for coffee, with knees drawn to my chest. I'm mesmerized by the consistency I notice in the water's motion. The new becomes time worn traveling its forerunner's path. When I change my focus from the current to the surface, sound is still and motion stops. A different world presents when action calms. I am not alone. A dance for life takes place above and below the water's surface, and along the stream's bed of sand and stone. Fish pursue plant debris. Big fish chase small fish that chase little fish. A few fish stalk flying insects that play a daring game of cat-and-mouse on the water's surface.

The supper hour is later today. Since dining in a rich environment is rare, I ring the dinner bell. Macaroni and cheese and Ramen noodles, with a Snickers bar for dessert are the menu selections this afternoon.

I'm hydrated and confident carrying a full load of energy producing calories when I finish my evening meal. I do not need my wristwatch to know it's time to pack and leave. The late afternoon sun is casting early shadows on the ravine walls. I'm ready to hike and the daylight is ending.

Today is October 8, 2013. Southbound thru-hikers continue to mention views from Albert Mountain's Fire Tower when we meet on the trail. Albert Mountain's summit is eight miles from this stream. I plan to eat lunch there, tomorrow. Tomorrow is my son, James' birthday. If I climb the mountain tonight, I'll have an excellent opportunity to photograph sunrise from the mountaintop for James' birthday gift.

I've climbed challenging Appalachian Mountains in Virginia, Georgia, and North Carolina. Georgia's mountains are the toughest. The sides are steep, and switchbacks are scarce. I ate lunch atop Standing Indian Mountain, North Carolina earlier today. The view at 5,500-feet elevation was worth the extra steps. I can climb Albert Mountain tonight.

As I pull on dry socks and boots, I decide to skip Carter Gap Shelter and try for the summit of Albert Mountain. My spirit-voice stirs with this change in plan:

Are you sure, Doug? Remember the last time we walked away from Partnership Shelter in the dark. We hiked flat terrain, and we were lucky we made it through the night to Trimpi Shelter. Albert is a mountain. Doug, we've never climbed a mountainside in the dark.

I'm sure I'll be just fine tonight, if I stay alert and work hard. These are facts from another day. I pick my rocks and one-two-three rapid jumps later; I land on dry ground with dry clothes and equipment. I follow Kirby Creek for a time before the Appalachian Trail heads up the Tennessee Valley Divide toward Albert Mountain.

Night climbs may be risky, but tomorrow is a day to celebrate. I delight the critters when I laugh aloud dwelling on this irony: James outlasted the mantel of excellence I placed on him at birth to celebrate this day with his family. I will get through tonight's climb to honor James' birth and celebrate the joy I receive each day I live with my son.

As dusk turns to early night, I glimpse at squirrels racing back and forth across the forest floor before they leap onto familiar tree trunks and snuggle in their nests. Safe in their homes, they watch me dance with my pack around a corner and out of their life.

My boots glide with the trail at a night pace. Adrenaline masks my fear. I am young and fearless tonight. I gain confidence acknowledging I can still tap into natural abilities that defined me during a different time of life.

My spirit voice speaks: *Doug, taking on Albert Mountain in daylight is a challenge. It's foolish climbing this mountainside in the dark of night.*

I ignore the fear held in this truth, adjust the headlamp beam, and embrace the goal to celebrate James' birthday at a place where darkness ends, and light begins. I'm excited more than I am afraid traveling alone in the deep wilderness tonight.

A star blanket and a bright moon shine nightlight through the tree canopy. I follow the trail contour by moonlight and my headlamp picks up white stripes painted on the trees that mark the Appalachian Trail for its hikers.

Insect noise keeps me company until the night sounds stop. Something has the insects' attention at Bearpen Gap. This sound of silence sends the chill of fear straight through me.

I slow my pace and concentrate where I place boot heels and then toes on the ground. My bear bell stops ringing. I move in silence on the footpath until it separates into two paths. Blue paint marks a tree. A water source is available on the side trail. I need water more than I sense danger.

I advance on the side trail until I hear water slurped. The sound reminds me of Buddy drinking from the toilet back home. The noise is comforting until I realize the sound is much louder than Buddy's water lap. Even at this late hour, it only takes a moment for me to envision the size of an animal that "out-slurps" Buddy: BIG BEAR.

Doug, we'll survive with one water bottle tonight, spirit-voice quickly chimes in. *Quietly remove us from this footpath.*

My inner-voice and I are finally in agreement today. I breathe when I hear water splashing in the opposite direction.

Night calm ends when I start the ascent to Albert Mountain Fire Tower. The incline is a physical and mental challenge. I am an older man who has never climbed a mountain alone in the dark. The night air captures my light and returns shadows that make it hard to assess depth and distance.

Am I afraid? No. Do I sense fear? Yes. Fear is a welcome hiking partner. Danger's presence triggers adrenaline I will depend on to keep my mind sharp and my muscles young.

The climb to Albert's summit is hours of treacherous steps. I must place my boot in the right location each time I lift my foot to lessen pain and limit the possibility of suffering harm. The risks are real. The danger is manageable if I am patient and stay alert.

I carefully work my way up Albert Mountain's rocky slopes, steep and jagged outcrops, and tight ledges. I am surprised when I break away from the rock trail's harsh ascent and enter a clearing filled with silhouettes of short trees and large bushes. Fifteen minutes later, I finish another small ascent, and to my complete surprise, I stop next to a steel framework anchored to large concrete pads. I tilt my head back and absorb the full length of Albert Mountain Fire Tower.

"Unbelievable. I executed a night climb to the Albert Mountain Fire Tower and stand next to the steel tower to tell the story," I say aloud to myself and no one else.

My climbing trance dissipates as I lean forward to lengthen my backpack's shoulder straps and unbuckle the chest and waist belts. I stand tall, bend my knees, and twist my torso to release my equipment. My backpack slides from my shoulder to my hand to the ground beside my feet.

Today's miles leave an impression: Standing Indian Mountain Summit, Ravine at Kirby Creek, Bearpen Gap, and Albert Mountain Fire Tower. The price paid for today's effort is obvious; both knees are the size of grapefruits. The reward rests before my eyes. A star blanket overlays a dark abyss that stretches from the mountain's edge to my imagination's limit.

The words, "Please, still my soul," slip from my lips without any conscious consideration.

I am here, Doug, whispers my inner-voice. *Concentrate when you take in this clean mountain air. Sense your soul waken with the rhythmic pace of your breathing. Listen to your heart beat. Wait with me for dawn to arrive.*

When you rise from your sleeping pad, search the sky for the space where the moon meets the sun. Watch for changing shades of dark and the first sprinkle of color in night's ending sky. Be attentive; you will witness IAM's unmistakable presence at daybreak.

"I will wait with you for dawn to arrive, spirit-voice," I promise.

I stretch my hands to the night sky. My muscles lengthen as they fight to keep their tension. I hold this pose in the mountain air, then reach higher to encourage tired muscles to release and relax. I groan, then chuckle acknowledging my pain: *thank you for reminding me the body of my youth is gone forever. You will not stop me, body pain. I will tolerate you to carry my pack to* places *others dream of enjoying while they sleep.*

A cup of hot chocolate sounds delicious, but I am conserving water until I reach Long Branch Shelter, tomorrow morning. I can't find a good place to set up my tent, so I drag my sleeping pad and bag under high bushes for protection.

When I finish writing to my grandchildren, I find my way to my sleeping place. Sleep does not come tonight. I rest, waiting for daybreak. I spend the nighttime hours lying on hard ground, wondering how water can drip from a cloudless sky through leaves of the brush canopy onto the tarp I use for shelter. Maybe someone will explain this phenomenon for me one day.

I rise early and climb the observation tower to reach the highest platform before dawn. When I sit, I discover the extent I abused my body yesterday. My lower body is swollen from my knees to my toes. Not to worry. I'll increase my Ibuprofen dosage and fix the underlying problem when I finish my journey.

Dawn announces with a pinprick. The tiny hole explodes, ripping the purple night with a jagged line of intense whites that mix with streaks of blending orange, red, and yellow. The crease erupts, elevating the purple night on rising steps of whites to blue's full spectrum of color. I am present to capture this phenomenon with my cell phone camera.

When the Appalachian Trail embraces open sky, I search for approaching thunderclouds. I track these blackish-gray super structures at eye level from ridge crest to ridge crest, hoping I beat the wind and lightning they store to the next shelter.

When sunlight fades on a mountain footpath, I quicken my pace to arrive at a clearing in time to see nature create art on evening sky.

I spend my lunch break with my head propped against my backpack, gazing at a ceiling painted multiple shades of deep blue. I view white figures float just above my eye level. Same as a snowflake, I have never seen two alike. Why do snowflakes fall to the ground and my lunch guests stay suspended above me and below the deeper blue sky?

Ground clouds frustrate me when their moisture is mixed with temperatures too warm to wear rain gear, but too cool for comfort. I travel in eerie silence through the varying walls of gray mist when these clouds shroud my path, jacket the vegetation, and dampen my clothes, boots, and equipment.

This morning, clouds break against the mountain sides the same as sea water slams against a rocky shoreline.

I listen to backcountry walkers with envy and polite attention when they share a life-altering moment they experience in solitude. This is my moment.

White energy bound in yellow power rises above the horizon, then blows through the mountain standing across the valley. Before I can lower my eyes, the sphere detonates in my world with white energy that catches me off guard. When I blink the sunspots away from my eyes, the horizon radiates white illumination. Albert Mountain radiates vibrant colors of greens, reds, yellows, and gold mixed with the nighttime's fading shadows.

When the sun rises to a distance equal to my hand palm and fingers, sunbeams stretch across the valley in a visible array of streaming light. I wait for the sun's rays to embrace me and remove the night cold from my body. As I watch, the clouds pull back from the mountainsides same as the tide draws oceans from coastlines. The atmosphere is breathing in moisture to rain on me during another time on the Appalachian Trail.

This explosive transformation from night to day affirms what I know is true: man makes, and IAM creates. The Creator reigns over this creation with a power worthy of my praise and my living faith.

Today is your birthday. Happy birthday to you, James!

Chapter Twenty-Four
Austin, Texas

When Buddy jumped into Maye's SUV at Springer Mountain and returned to Roanoke, the Appalachian Trail challenge morphed for me from an exciting adventure with my companion into a 300-mile endurance event filled with breathtaking scenery, tedious terrain, and physical pain I masked with high dosages of Ibuprofen. I will not ask you to throw away time reading pages, describing me walking these miles of trail in pain by myself. Let me say this: the fall season arrived in full force as I moved from Georgia to North Carolina and Northern Virginia. Temperatures dropped as foliage colors renewed to fading reds, oranges, golds, yellows, and then transformed to ground cover which concealed the pathway I followed every day.

Today is November 6, 2013; the day I walk off the Appalachian Trail at Harpers Ferry, West Virginia. I wake up before dawn, wondering if Daniel and Jordan have completed their thru-hike at Springer Mountain, Georgia by now. I haven't heard from my friends since they arrived in Damascus, Virginia. Jordan mentioned he planned to visit his sister in California when he left the trail. Daniel is a free spirit. He didn't have specific plans once he completed his thru-hike. He is probably singing at a coffeehouse in Georgia or North Carolina; waiting for his next life path to reveal itself.

I leave Bear's Den Hostel at daybreak and hike toward Buddy and Maye. They wait for me at a trailhead outside Harper's Ferry, West Virginia. Maye dresses to hike and they both have their hiking equipment ready in the SUV. I've promised them we will finish this year's hike backpacking together to the Maryland state line.

Buddy runs to my open arms when I break through the tree line. I sit on the ground to love my best friend before he knocks me to the ground.

"You're beautiful, Buddy-Boy. I missed you every day. Thank you for waiting for me."

My dog dances in circles and thumps me with his tail. He's healed and ready to play.

I slowly raise to my knees and I pull my overgrown puppy toward me.

"Sweet-Boy, I've given the wilderness everything I've got. Let's go home to our family."

Buddy sits, faces me nose to nose, and stares deep into my eyes before he licks my cheek. It's his way to say, *"I've missed you, too, Poppy. I go where you go. Let's go home."*

Maye watches me move to her. When she sees the pain I carry, she knows we aren't hiking today. I feel terrible. She works so hard for Buddy and me. I want to give her this gift.

"Jimmy Doug, you're in bad shape. When did you start suffering this level of pain?"

"Does it matter, Sweet-Friend?" I say with a smile, "I completed my goal. I'm standing with you and Buddy, today."

We visit the Appalachian Trail Conservancy the next morning, drive back to Roanoke where Buddy and I say goodbye to Adam and Maye, then we drive back to Texas. Saturday morning in Austin, Texas is special. My friends and I gather and run the footpath around Town Lake. My first Saturday back in town is no different. I am excited to see my friends and enjoy a fun run while we catch up on life missed. The last time we ran together, I was preparing to run the 10-mile Run for the Water race, the 3M Half Marathon, and the Austin Marathon. This morning, I am forced to walk 400 yards into the run. The body I bring back from the Appalachian Trail doesn't give me a choice.

I take yoga classes when I return; preparing my body to finish the second half of my Appalachian Trail thru-hike. Yoga teaches balance and focus. The class' token male is easy to spot. I'm the inflexible person trying to emulate a graceful woman.

I believe I execute basic poses same as a seasoned yoga disciple. In my mind, I stand feet shoulder-length apart and arms at the side with the best ladies in my class. I sit tall and lay flat on my back and stomach, the same as yoga professionals.

The challenge begins when I am asked to execute a yoga pose from a standing position. I tilt, wobble, and sometimes fall, depending on where I place my feet.

Do you laugh with me or cry for me if you take my class?

The hardest pose is Tree. The instructor and classmates move to one foot with a fluid motion and then place the other foot on their standing thigh. Participants center and balance, then move both palms to meet at a center point above their heads. When they conclude the pose, tree trunks are legs and tree branches are extended arms.

My balance betrays me before my floating foot touches my standing calf muscle. I am still trying to balance with my first foot when the class completes the entire exercise.

"Focus on my core and find my center," sounds good when an attractive instructor executing a perfect pose speaks the phrase.

These words are meaningless; absent the ability to stand on one foot. My mind cannot make my body execute the Tree pose. I have good excuses: 'healing injuries', 'inflexible muscles' and 'tendons', and 'a wandering mind', just to name a few.

The Appalachian Trail is a rough and tumble proposition for aging athletes. Visits to orthopedic surgeons, a foot specialist, a neurologist, and a neurosurgeon reveal my physical concerns are more challenging than these excuses. A broken big toe, a tumor on my heel, and arthritic knees are minor physical discomforts I bring back from the Appalachian Trail.

What I carried to the Appalachian Trail destroys my balance. A tumor fills my spinal column and surrounds my spinal cord from my middle back, beyond my spinal cord's end. The tumor chokes nerves that impact the lower leg and the foot functions. Now I know why I suffered the last 300-miles and why I could not move the toes on my right foot when I exited the last trailhead at Harper's Ferry, West Virginia. Douglas J. Fox, MD, a neurosurgeon in Austin, Texas performed a complicated and successful surgery to remove the tumor and prevent further damage to my nerves. Since I can't finish the second half of my thru-hike while I recover, I'm using this time to share my walk with Buddy with you.

What is my take away after living in solitude for 500-miles on the Appalachian Trail? It's simple: focus on my surroundings, not my circumstances. Time is finite, not infinite.

At age 62, these moments with nature still motivate me to work to return to the backcountry and finish what I start; walking the Appalachian Trail, from Springer Mountain, Georgia to Katahdin, Maine.

Epilogue

I backpack the Appalachian Mountains by myself, confident I do not walk alone. The spirits of individuals who traveled this land before me linger: Native Americans, explorers, pioneers, settlers, homesteaders, and backcountry walkers; men, women, and children who lived, survived, and pushed onward before my day.

Take on these mighty struggles alone, and you will learn to trust your ability to overcome unknowns in any situation. Rise with dawn and make ready for bed with the sunset. Dream while you wait for the new day to appear. Dance across steps created in earth and rock by sojourners and animals alike. Eat when you are hungry and drink when fresh water is handy. Speak to good souls when they join you for an hour or a day.

Nature speaks in the wilderness' solitude. Listen and discover for yourself forerunner's truth: your time is finite not infinite. How you make life decisions matters. Wisdom rarely presents itself in isolation; acting on channeled thoughts scribed by a person representing a higher authority or a celestial entity. Truth manifests honoring life failures when interacting with people from different backgrounds, cultures, and religions. The best choice may force you to set aside worries and find contentment in the discomfort of immediate circumstance.

Begin anew when you absorb nature's gift. Be patient walking in solitude or marching as one with many, and you can experience what others only dream.

Other Photographs Available Upon Request.